"Do you know why t̶ after you?"

"I'm still not sure."

"We'll figure it out."

He clasped her to him, holding her in place, and she was content to lie on top of him, still marveling at the way they had traveled together to an undiscovered country.

"This is what we were meant for," he murmured, absolute conviction in his voice.

She understood what he was saying.

Always incomplete.

Until now.

"Why did it happen?" she asked.

"We have to find out," he said as he stroked her arm.

She gave a short laugh. "You're saying we can't just enjoy it."

"Is that what you want to do?"

She considered the question. "No. I want to understand. And of course, we still have to figure out why those men want to question me—then kill me."

DIAGNOSIS: ATTRACTION

USA TODAY Bestselling Author

REBECCA YORK

(Ruth Glick writing as Rebecca York)

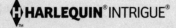

HARLEQUIN® INTRIGUE®

Recycling programs
for this product may
not exist in your area.

ISBN-13: 978-0-373-69757-1

DIAGNOSIS: ATTRACTION

Copyright © 2014 by Ruth Glick

This edition published by arrangement with Harlequin Books S.A.

For questions and comments about the quality of this book, please contact us at CustomerService@Harlequin.com.

® and TM are trademarks of Harlequin Enterprises Limited or its corporate affiliates. Trademarks indicated with ® are registered in the United States Patent and Trademark Office, the Canadian Trade Marks Office and in other countries.

Printed in U.S.A.

ABOUT THE AUTHOR

Award-winning, *USA TODAY* bestselling novelist Ruth Glick, who writes as Rebecca York, is the author of more than one hundred books, including her popular 43 Light Street series for the Harlequin Intrigue line. Ruth says she has the best job in the world. Not only does she get paid for telling stories, she's also an author of twelve cookbooks. Ruth and her husband, Norman, travel frequently, researching locales for her novels and searching out new dishes for her cookbooks.

Books by Rebecca York

HARLEQUIN INTRIGUE
706—PHANTOM LOVER*
717—INTIMATE STRANGERS*
745—BOYS IN BLUE
         "Jordan"
765—OUT OF NOWHERE*
783—UNDERCOVER ENCOUNTER
828—SPELLBOUND*
885—RILEY'S RETRIBUTION
912—THE SECRET NIGHT*
946—CHAIN REACTION
994—ROYAL LOCKDOWN
1017—RETURN OF THE WARRIOR*
1072—SOLDIER CAGED*
1089—CHRISTMAS SPIRIT
1150—MORE THAN A MAN*
1187—POWERHOUSE
1215—GUARDING GRACE
1256—SOLID AS STEELE*
1327—SUDDEN INSIGHT**
1332—SUDDEN ATTRACTION**
1375—HER BABY'S FATHER
1435—CARRIE'S PROTECTOR
1484—BRIDAL JEOPARDY**
1490—DIAGNOSIS: ATTRACTION**

*43 Light Street
**Mindbenders

CAST OF CHARACTERS

Elizabeth Forester—Her memories were missing until Dr. Matthew Delano touched her.

Matt Delano—Would his strong sense of right and wrong keep him from having a personal relationship with a patient?

Polly Kramer—Did she make a fatal mistake by helping Elizabeth?

Derek Lang—First he had to find Elizabeth, then he had to question her and kill her.

Gary Southwell—He was just doing his job—until it became personal.

Sabrina—She'd stopped trusting Elizabeth, but she needed her help.

Harold Goddard—Why did he fear Matt and Elizabeth?

Thomas Harrison—The police detective was searching for Matt and Elizabeth.

Tony Verrazano—What happened to his memory when he ran into Matt and Elizabeth?

Mrs. Vivian—Was she a key player in Derek Lang's criminal enterprise or just an obedient employee?

Chapter One

Panic choked off Elizabeth Forester's breath as she turned the car onto Mulberry Street, the wheels screeching when she took the corner too fast. The maneuver didn't shake the car that was following her. She was pretty sure she had picked up the tail after she had left the motel where she'd been hiding out—using a car she thought nobody would recognize. She made a snorting sound. Apparently her precautions hadn't been enough.

For the past week, she'd been acting like she was in the middle of a TV cop show. But she'd decided the evasive action was necessary. Today it looked like she'd been absolutely right to try to cover her tracks.

It had gradually dawned on her that a dark-blue Camaro was appearing in her rearview mirror on a regular basis—following her during the day—and that the ever-present car must be connected to the case she was working on. Something too big for her to handle?

She hadn't started off understanding how big it really was. But a lot of little details had led her to the conclusion that she needed to protect herself by checking into the motel a few miles from her house and taking alternate routes to work.

She glanced again in the rearview mirror. The blue car was inching up, and she could see two tough-looking men in the front seat. She shuddered, imagining what they were going to do if they got their hands on her.

She'd almost decided to go to the police with what she

knew at this point, until she'd concluded that the plan was dangerous. It was terrible when you couldn't trust the authorities, but she had to assume that they were protecting the man who'd sent the thugs to intercept her.

As her work took her all over Baltimore, she had an excellent knowledge of the city. If she could get far enough ahead of the men tailing her, she could turn into the nest of alleys up ahead and disappear. And then what? For now the prime objective was to get away.

She made another quick turn into an alley, slowing her Honda in case a kid came darting out from one of the fenced-in backyards.

Glancing behind her, she breathed out a little sigh. She was in the clear. In the next moment, she realized her mistake as she saw the Camaro whip around the corner also. Damn.

Still on the lookout for pedestrians, she sped up again, turning onto the next street. To her horror, a delivery van had just pulled over to the curb. And a car coming in the other direction made it impossible to escape by crossing to that lane.

She swerved to avoid the van, thinking she could squeeze past on the sidewalk. But a woman and a little boy were coming straight toward her.

The fear on their faces as they saw the car bearing down on them made her gasp as she swerved again. If a lamppost hadn't suddenly materialized in front of her, she could have gotten away. But she plowed into it and came to a rocking stop.

The old Honda she was driving didn't have an air bag. The seat belt kept her from hitting the windshield, but she was stunned as she sat behind the wheel.

She knew she had to escape on foot, but she was moving slowly now. Before she could get out of the car, one of the men from the Camaro appeared at her window.

"Got ya, bitch."

Yanking open the car door, he dragged her out, hitting her

head on the car frame as he hurled her to the sidewalk. The
blow stunned her, and then everything went black.

DR. MATTHEW DELANO's first stop on his morning rounds
was the computer at the nurses' station, where he scanned
for urgent cases and noted which patients had been discharged—or had passed away—since his last visit to the
internal-medicine floor.

No deaths. He always counted that as a good sign. This
morning most of the patients on the general-medicine floor
were in for routine problems—except for one woman whom
the cops had named Jane Doe because she didn't remember who she was.

As he read the notes from the E.R., he gathered that the
whole situation with her was odd. For starters, she hadn't
been carrying any identification. And she'd been driving an
old car registered to a Susan Swinton.

But when a patrol officer had knocked on Swinton's door
late in the afternoon yesterday, nobody had been home, and
the neighbors had said the woman was on an extended trip
out of the country. Which left the authorities with no clue as
to the identity of the mystery woman in room twenty-two.

Matt noted the irony of the room number. As in *Catch-22*,
the novel by Joseph Heller. The term had come to mean a par-
adoxical situation in which a person is trapped by conflicting
circumstances beyond his control.

Dr. Delano skimmed the chart. The woman, who was apparently in her late twenties, had no physical injuries, except
for a bump on the head. The MRI showed she'd had a mild
concussion, but that was resolving itself. The main problem
was her missing memory—leading to her unknown identity.

Her trouble intrigued him. But although he was curious
to see what she looked like, he made his way methodically
down the hall, checking on patients on a first-come-first-
served basis. A woman with COPD. A man with a bladder

infection he couldn't shake. Another man with advanced Parkinson's disease.

They were all routine cases for Dr. Delano since spending time in a dangerous African war zone a couple months ago and taking this interim job in Baltimore, where at least he could feel useful.

He hadn't really wanted to return to the States—he was more comfortable in a foreign country than at home. Here he had to do normal stuff when he wasn't working, and normal stuff was never his first choice.

He liked the rough-and-tumble life of doctoring in a war zone and the chance to help people in desperate need of medical attention. But now the rebels were systematically shooting any outsiders who were dumb enough to stay in their country and try to help the people. Since Matt wasn't suicidal, he was back in Baltimore, working at Memorial Hospital while he figured out the best way to serve humanity.

He made a soft snorting sound as he walked down the hall, thinking that was a lofty way to put it, especially for a man who felt disconnected from people. But he'd become an expert at faking it. In fact, he was often praised for his excellent bedside manner.

He stopped at the door to room twenty-two, feeling a sense of anticipation and at the same time reluctance. Shaking that off, he raised his hand and knocked.

"Come in," a feminine voice called.

When he stepped into the room, the woman in the bed zeroed in on him, her face anxious. He stopped short, studying her from where he stood eight feet away.

She wore no makeup and the standard hospital gown. Her short dark hair was tousled, and she had a nasty bruise on her forehead, but despite her disarray, he found her very appealing, from her large blue eyes to her well-shaped lips and the small, slightly upturned nose.

She looked to be in her late twenties as her chart had

estimated. About his own age, he judged. She sat forward, fixing her gaze on him with a kind of unnerving desperation.

"Hello," he said. "I'm Dr. Delano."

"I'd say pleased to meet you, if I knew how to introduce myself," she answered.

"I take it you're still having memory problems?"

"Unfortunately. I don't know who I am or what happened to me."

"It says in your chart that you were in a one-car accident."

"They told me that part. Apparently I hit a light pole. It's the rest of it that's a mystery." She gave her arm a little flap of exasperation. "I don't know why I didn't have a purse. The cops said there was a crowd around me, and a man had pulled me out of the car. The best I can figure is that he took the purse and disappeared." She dragged in a breath and let it out. "I don't even know if the man is somebody I know—or just a random thief taking advantage of a woman who had an accident. Either way, I don't like it. He left me in a heck of a fix."

"I understand," Matt answered, keying in on her fears. Some pretty scary things had happened to him in his overseas travels. In one African country, he'd been threatened with having his arms cut off—or worse—until he'd volunteered to remove some bullets from a bunch of rebels.

He'd been shot at too many times to count. And he'd been on a plane that had made an almost-crash landing on a dirt runway of a little airport out in the middle of nowhere. Taking all that into consideration, he still wouldn't like to be in this woman's shoes. She had no money. No memory. Nowhere to stay when she got out of the hospital.

She must have seen his reaction.

"Sorry to be such a bother."

"That's not what I was thinking."

"Then what?"

"I was feeling sorry for you, if you must know."

"Right. I'm trying to keep from having a panic attack."

He tipped his head to the side. "You know what that means—panic attack?"

"Yes. You get shaky. Your heart starts to pound." She laughed. "And you feel like you're going to die."

"You remember details like that but not who you are?"

"I guess that must be true."

"Have you ever had one?"

That stopped her. "Either I have or I've read about it."

"Is the picture of the syndrome vivid in your mind?"

"Yes."

"So it's probably more than just reading about the subject. Either you had one or you know someone who has."

Her gaze turned inward, and he knew she was trying to remember which it was.

"Your chart says you're doing okay physically. Let's have a look at you."

She sighed. "Okay."

"Does anything hurt?"

"The lump on my head is still painful—but tolerable."

"Good."

"And I'm kind of stiff—from the impact."

"Understandable. Let's check your pupillary reflexes."

She tipped her face up, and he looked into one eye and then the other with the flashlight, noting that the pupils were contracting normally.

"Okay, that's good. I'm going to check your heart and lungs." He pressed the stethoscope against her chest, listening to her steady heartbeat. "Good."

Up until then it had been a routine examination—or as routine as it could be when the patient had amnesia. When he put a hand on her arm, everything changed.

As he touched her, she gasped as though an electric current had shot through her, and perhaps he did too, because suddenly the room began to whirl around him, making it seem like the two of them were in the center of a private, invisible tornado. He knew the windows hadn't blown in or anything. The air in the room was perfectly still, as it had been moments before. The whirling was all in his mind. And hers because he was picking up on her confusion and sense of disorientation—as well as his own.

He should let go of her, but he felt as though he was riveted in place. With his hand on her arm, memories leaped toward him. Her memories—that she'd said were inaccessible to her. He was sure she hadn't been lying, but somehow recollections that had been unavailable to her were flooding into his consciousness.

The first thing he knew for sure was that her name wasn't Jane Doe. It was Elizabeth something. He clenched his teeth, struggling to catch the last name, but it seemed to be dangling just beyond his reach. Although he couldn't get it, he latched on to a whole series of scenes from her past.

Elizabeth as a little girl, at her first day of nursery school—shy, uncertain and then panicked, watching Mommy leave her alone in a roomful of children she didn't know. Elizabeth as a grade-schooler working math problems from a textbook. Elizabeth refusing to eat the beef tongue her mother had bought—to save grocery money.

Elizabeth alone in her room, reading a book about two lovers and wishing she could have the same feelings for someone. Elizabeth leaving the hockey field, distraught because she'd missed making a goal she thought should have been hers. And then in a college classroom—taking a social studies exam and sure she was going to get a perfect score.

The old memories faded and were replaced by something much more recent. From yesterday. She was worried about being followed. She was driving an old car she'd borrowed from a friend, glancing frequently in the rearview mirror—seeing a blue vehicle keeping pace with her.

She sped up, fleeing the pursuers, weaving down alleys

and onto the street again. She thought she was going to get away until a delivery van had blocked her escape. She plowed into a lamppost with a bone-jarring impact. While she was still stunned from the crash, a man rushed to her, yanking her from the car, hitting her head on the door frame as he pulled her onto the sidewalk, just as a crowd of onlookers gathered.

"Hey, what are you doing to her?" somebody had demanded.

That memory of the accident cut off abruptly with a flash of pain in her head and neck. She must have passed out, and one of the people who'd come running had called 9-1-1.

The recollections flowing from her mind to his were like pounding waves, but they weren't the only thing he experienced. As he made the physical connection with her, he felt an overwhelming sexual pull that urged him to do more than dip into her thoughts.

He was her doctor, which meant that ethically there could be nothing personal between the two of them; yet he couldn't stop himself from gathering her close. Somewhere in his own mind he couldn't squelch the notion that letting go of her would be like his own death.

And he knew from her thoughts that she felt the same powerful connection to him. It made her feel desperate. Aroused. More off-balance than either one of them had ever been in their lives.

He told himself he should pull away. But he was trapped where he was, because her arms came up to wrap around his waist. Well, not trapped. He wanted to be here, and she'd given him a reason not to break the connection.

She pressed herself against him, increasing the contact and the frustration and the sheer need. He breathed in her scent, picturing himself bending down so that he could lower his mouth to hers, imagining the taste of her and letting himself see what it would be like to kick off his shoes and climb into the hospital bed with her.

She made a small needy sound, and he knew that she was picturing the same thing as he was. Part of his mind was shocked and aghast at how far he was going with this fantasy. The other part ached to push her back onto the bed and roll on top of her so he could press his body to hers. Only first he needed to drag off his shirt and pants and get rid of her hospital gown.

That last frantic image was what finally made him come to his senses and pull away, breaking the physical contact and, at the same time, the mental connection.

He stood beside the bed, dragging in lungsful of air, feeling dizzy and disoriented and still achingly aroused.

And she was staring at him, looking like a woman who was ready for sex. When she reached out her hand toward him, he forced himself to step farther back.

He cursed under his breath, ordering himself not to think about making love with her, as he clawed his way toward rational behavior. For a few moments, he'd felt an overwhelming connection with Elizabeth—even though he was sure he'd never met her before. But he did know that she was a patient, and thinking about anything physical between them was completely out of bounds. It was morally wrong, and it could get him in big trouble, come to that.

Which left him trying to understand what had happened between the two of them in those seconds when they were touching. Both the flood of memories from her mind and the sudden intense sexual attraction that had threatened to wipe any reasonable thoughts from his mind.

He shook his head as he gazed down on her. She sat on the bed, looking stunned, her blue eyes wide, her breath coming in little gasps as she clenched and unclenched her fingers on the sheet.

"I'm sorry," he managed to say.

"Are you?"

"Of course. That was completely inappropriate."

"I think it took both of us by surprise," she said, making an excuse.

"You're a patient."

Ignoring the observation, she said, "What happened?"

"I don't know."

"Touching you made me recall things I couldn't remember for myself. And I got inside your mind, too. I didn't know a thing about you before we touched. Now I know you always went in for dangerous sports. Like mountain climbing. Spelunking. And ice camping."

"Yeah."

"Why?"

"They made me feel alive," he said, unaccountably admitting something to this woman that he had always kept to himself.

"And recently you were in Africa. In the middle of a nasty little war. They were shooting at you, and the guy next to you was killed. You stayed hidden, with him on top of you, soaking your clothes with his blood, until it got dark and you could sneak away."

He answered with a small wordless nod. It was something he'd tried to forget, and she'd pulled it from his memories.

"You went there to help people, and you saved a lot of lives. But you never knew quite how to connect with anyone." She gulped. "Just like me."

The admission jolted him. "What do you mean?"

She kept her gaze fixed on him. "You were in my head. You know I'm like you, with that feeling of not being able to…relate to people on the deep level you crave. Like everybody else has a secret handshake, only nobody ever taught it to you."

He'd never thought of it quite that way, but he nodded, because she had spoken the truth. All his adult life—all his life, really—he'd been searching for something he was sure he could not find. Something other people had, but he lacked.

Until now, with this woman. But that couldn't be possible—not after all the years of being alone.

"Why you?" he whispered.

"I don't know."

"Because you can't remember your past?"

"What would that have to do with it?"

He shrugged. "I don't know."

"But touching you brought back memories I couldn't reach a few minutes ago," she said again.

He nodded.

"Let's take it from the opposite angle. Why you?" she murmured.

"I have no idea."

Neither one of them seemed capable of looking away from the other. But he took another step from her, because he was so off-kilter that he wasn't sure what to do. Maybe something crazy like reach for her again, because touching her had been like every aching fantasy he'd ever experienced.

She moistened her lips. "What exactly happened?"

"I don't know. But I found out that your name is Elizabeth."

She gave a nervous laugh. "I have amnesia, but when you touched me, you brought some of my memories back."

"Yes."

"Did that ever happen to you before?" she asked.

"No. To you?"

"No." She laughed again. "At least I don't think so. The only personal things I remember are what you gave me."

There was no logic to what she'd just said. And she might have been lying. But he didn't think so.

He saw the challenge in her eyes and heard it in her voice. "We could try it again. Maybe you can bring back more of me."

"I can't."

"Even when I'm alone and desperate?" she asked in a low voice.

Her words and the pleading look in her eyes made his throat tighten. More than that, when he touched her, he sensed that she was a good person. She didn't deserve what had happened to her, although he knew objectively that being good or bad didn't have anything to do with what people endured.

Like the guy next to him getting shot. Jerry had been a good person, too. But anyone could lead an exemplary life and end up being killed by a stray bullet that came through the living-room wall.

Dr. Delano pushed the disturbing images out of his mind and managed to say, "It wasn't just memories. At least for me. There was another aspect to it."

He saw her flush. "Not just memories," she agreed, then looked down at her hands. "Sexual arousal," she whispered.

"But that was completely inappropriate. I'm your doctor. There can't be anything personal between us."

She took her lower lip between her teeth. "Even if your touching me makes me remember? I mean, isn't that…medically beneficial?"

"I'm afraid I can't stretch the definition that far."

She played with the edge of the sheet again, pleating it between her thumb and finger. "That last scene—where the guy dragged me out of the car. I don't think he was trying to help me. He looked relieved to have caught up with me— but not in a good way."

"I think that's right."

"I think he was following me, and I was trying to get away. That's why I crashed into a lamppost. I was desperate to escape from him and the other guy—the one who was driving."

"Do you remember it that way?"

Frustration flared in her eyes. "Not on my own. I think that's what you picked up from me, right?"

He nodded.

"So, odd as it sounds, it must be true, because you saw what I couldn't."

"Yeah."

"Probably it would be a good idea to avoid running into him again. If I knew who he was and why he wanted to hurt me."

"Yes."

Her eyes narrowed. "You sound like a computerized therapy program, agreeing with everything I'm saying but not adding anything—besides what you pulled out of my head."

He felt his chest constrict. "I'm sorry."

"How am I going to stay out of that guy's clutches when I don't even know who I am or who he is?"

He wanted to help her, but his hands were tied because of the professional demeanor that he was forced to maintain. In the end, all he could say was, "I'm sorry. I don't know."

He stopped talking when he realized Elizabeth was staring at someone standing in the doorway behind him.

Chapter Two

Matt turned to see that Polly Kramer, one of the nurses, had come into the room behind him.

"Dr. Delano."

"Yes," he answered, relieved that someone else had intervened to break up the intensity of the encounter between him and Elizabeth but also wondering how much of the conversation the nurse had heard.

She must have picked up on something, perhaps the tone of their voices, because she asked, "Is there some problem?"

He was wondering what to say when Elizabeth answered from the bed. "Basically, still my memory." She cleared her throat. "But while Dr. Delano was examining me, a name popped into my head. I think it's my real name."

The woman's face lit up. "Why, that's marvelous. What is it?"

"Elizabeth." She waited a beat. "I only got the first name."

"But that's a start."

"I was hoping that Dr. Delano could help me dredge up some other facts about myself."

Kramer looked at him. "Can you help her?"

"I'm afraid not. The name came to her. It wasn't anything I did," he protested, not sure that he was actually telling the truth but totally unwilling to explain. He'd done something, but he'd only touched her, and he wasn't going to do it again.

The nurse nodded, then changed the subject. "Is Elizabeth ready to be discharged?"

"If I knew where to send her," Matt muttered. "Nobody's come forward looking for her?"

"I'm afraid not."

His gaze flicked to the woman on the bed, and they were probably both thinking, given her memory of the aftermath of the crash, that might be an advantage.

"Do you have any suggestions?" Elizabeth asked.

"I might," Nurse Kramer murmured, shifting her weight from one foot to the other.

Matthew waited for her to say what was on her mind.

After a long pause, the nurse said, "I have a spare room that I haven't used since my daughter got married and moved away. I was thinking that…Elizabeth might want to stay with me until she remembers who she is."

IN HIS DULANEY VALLEY mansion, Derek Lang leaned back in the comfortable leather chair behind his desk. He was a tall man, and the expensive chair was specially designed with a comfortable headrest. His dark hair was tamed by a four-hundred-dollar haircut. His well-muscled frame was clothed in a thousand-dollar suit. And he was currently having a facial massage administered by Susanna, one of the gorgeous young women he kept around the house. He liked them to have useful skills, in addition to being good in bed. And Susanna was a perfect example.

When she finished and stepped away, he picked up a hand mirror and inspected his face. At forty-five he still looked fit—because he took good care of himself with daily sessions in the gym on the weight machines and ellipticals. And he'd also had some nips and tucks by one of the most expensive plastic surgeons in the city.

"Thank you, honey," he murmured.

"You're welcome, Mr. Lang."

He gave her a long look as he thought about asking her to take off her halter top and miniskirt. Per his instructions, she wouldn't be wearing anything under either one, and she could stand in front of him while he ran his hands over her. Then he could pursue a couple of interesting alternatives. Like having her kneel in front of him. Or having her sit with her legs open at the edge of the desk.

Enjoying her services was a tempting prospect, but he had some urgent business to take care of. He flicked his eyes to her face, knowing she was following his thoughts and waiting for him to make a decision. He liked the power he had over her and everyone else who worked for him—either voluntarily or involuntarily. Susanna was one of the latter, of course.

He repressed a sigh. Business before pleasure. "Tell Southwell to come in."

"Yes, sir."

As she turned away, he patted her butt, then pulled his chair up to the desk. Moments later one of his best men entered and stood respectfully in front of the desk.

Gary Southwell had been a high-school football star, and Derek had recruited Gary at the end of his senior year because of his bulk and menacing appearance. Since appearance wasn't enough, Derek had Gary specially trained both in martial arts and on the firing range.

The man was adept at hand-to-hand combat and was an excellent shot. And he was grateful for the good salary he earned, the comfortable accommodations and the women he could shag anytime he wanted. All of that made him loyal to a fault. And anxious to please.

"Do we have a report on the Elizabeth Forester situation? Is she still in the hospital?" Derek asked. His men had been keeping tabs on her for weeks and closing in for the kill when she had wrecked her car, drawing too much attention from witnesses. Derek didn't like it when his plans went sour.

"She's still in the hospital," Southwell answered. "Her

physical condition is okay, but they're keeping her because she's lost her memory."

"You think that's true?"

Southwell shrugged.

"If it is, I wonder if it's because she'd rather not remember," Derek mused.

"That could be part of it," Southwell agreed. "And it's good for us, isn't it?"

"At the moment, but how long is that going to last?" Derek Lang asked.

"No way of knowing."

"If the memory loss were permanent, that would solve our problem. But I don't want her suddenly remembering why she's been so busy over the past few weeks and then calling in the cops."

"She didn't do it before."

"Because she knew that was dangerous, but getting hit on the head could have affected her judgment which could make her reckless now."

Southwell nodded.

"You went to her house after the accident," Derek said. "Anything I should know about?"

"We tore the place apart and didn't find anything on paper, but there were computer files with information you wouldn't want anyone to read."

Derek sat forward. "And?"

"We took out her hard drive and smashed it."

"Good. But that's not enough. We have to shut the woman up for good."

Southwell waited for instructions.

"I understand why Patterson couldn't get to her earlier," Derek said, thinking aloud. "There were too many people around the crash scene, asking her questions, trying to figure out who she was. Wait until the shift change at the hospital. They don't have as many people on at night."

"Got it."

He considered his options. "I don't want you to take care of her there. I mean, she's in a hospital, and we could get into trouble with the cause of death. Bring her to me. I'd like to ask her some questions about why she's been nosing around in my business, starting with what put her on to me in the first place. Maybe I can think of something that will jog her memory."

"Yes, sir."

Southwell left, and Derek leaned back in his chair, thinking of the methods he'd use in his basement interrogation room. In the movies, tough guys held out against torture. In reality, everybody ended up spilling their guts. And he was pretty sure that with a woman like Elizabeth Forester, it wouldn't take long. After he got what he needed, he'd have some fun with her before he killed her.

ELIZABETH'S HEART LEAPED at the offer from Mrs. Kramer, but she still forced herself to ask, "Are you sure it wouldn't be an imposition?"

"Of course not, dear."

"Thank you."

The woman had just solved one of her biggest problems—by offering a place to stay. But there was still the basic problem, with totally unexpected complications.

She'd been lying in this hospital bed trying to dredge up a memory—any memory—until the man standing across the room had put a hand on her, and everything had changed. At least for the few moments when they'd been touching.

She had a little sliver of herself back, courtesy of Dr. Delano's touch. Now she recalled the first day of nursery school. Playing field hockey. What had seemed like a college classroom.

Of course there was the little problem of the sexual arousal that had flared between them. His and hers. But she understood that he was a man with high moral standards, and he wasn't going to let himself get dragged into an inappropriate relationship with a female patient, which was why he'd flat-out refused to touch her again.

He'd opened a door in her mind just a crack and slammed it shut again. She'd alternated between being angry that he wouldn't help her and wanting to plead with him to give her more of herself back. But she'd understood where he was coming from and had kept from embarrassing herself any further.

Then that nice nurse who had taken care of her earlier had showed up and thrown her a lifeline to deal with her present day-to-day situation.

"I'd be very grateful to stay with you, but I insist on paying you—as soon as I find out who I am. I mean, assuming I'm not indigent or something."

"You're too well cared for to be indigent," the doctor said. "It's obvious that you were living at least a middle-class lifestyle."

"Okay." She looked from him to the nurse, wanting to be absolutely sure the woman had thought through her offer. "You're certain it's all right?"

"I'd love the company."

The doctor left, and the arrangement was settled quickly. Probably the hospital was anxious to get rid of a patient who couldn't produce an insurance card, even if she was living a middle-class lifestyle.

"I'm going off shift in half an hour," Mrs. Kramer said. "Once you get dressed, I'll get a wheelchair and take you down. I can meet you in the waiting area near the elevator."

Climbing out of bed, Elizabeth stood for a moment holding on to the rail. She'd been lying down too long, and her legs felt rubbery. Or maybe that was the result of having a concussion.

When she felt steadier on her feet, she crossed to the small bathroom and turned on the light. She'd deliberately avoided looking at herself until she was ready. Now she raised her gaze to the mirror and stared at the woman she saw there. She wasn't sure what she had expected, but the face that stared back might as well have belonged to a stranger.

Disappointed and unsettled, she stood for a moment, composing herself. Trying not to look in the mirror again, she washed her face at the sink and brushed her teeth with the toothbrush the hospital had provided.

Doggedly she focused on the simple tasks in order to keep from thinking about anything more stressful—like how she was going to figure out who she was and why she had crashed her car. The easy answer was that she'd been speeding. As she pictured herself driving, she realized she knew the part of town where they'd told her the accident had occurred.

That stopped her. She'd come up with another memory—this time on her own. Well, not a memory of anything personal.

The observation about Baltimore—that was the city she was in—brought up another question: What else did she know? Maybe not about Elizabeth Doe specifically but about the world around her.

She stopped and asked herself some questions she imagined would be standard for someone in her situation. She couldn't dredge up the correct date. But she knew who was president. And she knew... She struggled for another concrete fact and came up with the conviction that she could make scrambled eggs that tasted a lot better than what the hospital had served her this morning.

"Your clothes are in the closet," Nurse Kramer said through the bathroom door. "Do you need help?"

"I think I can do it myself," she said, because she wasn't going to depend on other people if there was a chance for independence—even in small things.

By the time she stepped back into the room, Mrs. Kramer had gone back to her duties and Dr. Delano wasn't there, either. She felt a stab of disappointment but brushed it aside. Probably he was wishing that some other doctor had examined her. And staying as far away as possible from her was probably the way to go, from his point of view.

After crossing to the closet, she took out the clothes that someone had hung up for her. Dark slacks. A white shirt and a dark jacket. A very buttoned-up look, except that the outfit was a little scuffed around the edges from the accident.

She looked at the labels of the garments. They were from good department stores. Not top-of-the-line but good enough. Another piece of information that she found interesting.

She'd been wearing knee-high stockings and black pumps with a wedge heel. Not the shoes she'd wear if she had wanted to impress someone. These were no-nonsense footwear. Did that mean she walked a lot as part of her job? Or maybe she had bad feet.

There was also underwear on the hanger, and that was more interesting than the exterior clothing. She'd been wearing a very sexy white lace bra and matching bikini panties. Apparently she liked to indulge in very feminine underwear. She took everything back into the bathroom, then decided that she might as well take a shower before she left. It would feel good to get clean. Too bad she didn't have a change of underwear.

She thought about her name as she stood under the shower. *Elizabeth.* A very formal name. Did people call her Beth? Betty? Liz? Or any of the other variations of the name? She didn't know.

But she noted that she'd washed her hair before soaping her body, and it had been in the back of her mind that she'd better do that first—in case the hot water went off and she was caught with shampoo in her hair.

An interesting priority. Did it mean she lived in a house

or an apartment where there was a problem with the hot-water heater? Or had she traveled abroad like Dr. Delano?

She clenched her hand around a bar of soap, annoyed with herself for switching her thoughts back to him. He'd made it clear that there couldn't be anything personal between the two of them, and she understood that. Yet, at the same time, she couldn't stop thinking of him as her lifeline to her own past.

After turning off the water and stepping out of the shower, she reached for a towel and began to dry herself. There was no hair dryer, so she worked extra hard on her hair, rubbing it into fluffy ringlets.

Was that the way she usually wore it? She didn't think so, but it would do for now. Her coiffure was way down on her list of priorities. It didn't matter what she looked like if she didn't know who she was and how she'd gotten herself into deep *kimchi.* Because it was clear from the memory Dr. Delano had dredged up that she'd done something to bring trouble on herself. Was it something she deserved? Or something that wasn't her fault?

She made a small sound of frustration as she tried to work around the holes in her memory, then stopped and started again. It was more like her entire past was a great void—except for the memories Matt Delano had brought to the surface. With that nagging side effect he hated, she reminded herself.

Well, that probably wasn't true. She was pretty sure he didn't hate the sexual pull between them. He'd responded, after all, but he was determined not to cross a line with her.

She clenched her fists in frustration. If she couldn't fill in all the blank places in her mind, they were going to drive her crazy.

Chapter Three

At the nurses' station, Matt was thinking about the moral issue that was tearing at him. Because he was very conscious of the sexual awareness between himself and Elizabeth Doe, he should stay away from her. But at the same time, how could he refuse to help her?

Mrs. Kramer came down the hall, her strides purposeful, and he looked up questioningly when he found her standing in front of him.

"Yes?"

"Do you get the feeling that Elizabeth is in some kind of trouble?" she asked. "I mean not just the memory loss."

"Yes."

"Perhaps she was fleeing from someone. There was a report of a man dragging her out of her car at the accident scene. Maybe he took her purse."

Matt nodded.

"Would it be all right, do you think, if I didn't tell anyone that I was taking her home with me? Well, I mean, anyone besides you."

"If someone is looking for her, wouldn't that make it harder to locate her?" he said.

"But I'm thinking, it's likely to be the wrong kind of person, and it might be better for him not to find her."

"Or it could be her husband, frantic for information."

"You think she's married?" Kramer asked.

"No," he answered immediately, then tried to assess his

firm conviction. His certainty came from her mind, but he couldn't tell that to Kramer. Instead, he said, "No ring."

As the nurse nodded, he took his private speculation a step further. The best he could figure was that he hadn't gotten any hint of a husband from her memories. Or any indication of a current relationship. Just from that brief trip into her mind, he thought that she was like him—disconnected from any meaningful relationship. Only for a few moments, the two of them had connected in a way he'd thought impossible for himself.

He clenched his teeth.

"Is something wrong?" Kramer asked.

Quickly he rearranged his features. "No."

"You look tense."

He wished she hadn't noticed.

When he didn't speak, the nurse said, "I'll let you know how she's doing."

"Thanks."

He did care, more than he should, but he couldn't admit it or anything else that would give away the out-of-kilter personal involvement that had flared between them. He turned and left the ward before Elizabeth came out, and he did something he knew he shouldn't—like touch her again.

Thinking about it made his nerve endings tingle, but he ignored the sensation as he headed for the other end of the hall.

POLLY KRAMER WATCHED Dr. Delano stride off. She could tell he was trying to react on a strictly professional level, but he wasn't succeeding. Which was interesting. Since he'd come to Memorial Hospital, she'd thought of him as closed up. Maybe even a cold fish. But something about the woman with no memory had created a change in him. He seemed to really care about her, although he was trying not to show it.

Probably he thought any personal feelings about Elizabeth were inappropriate. But was there some way to change that? He'd been cautious of involvement with her because she was a patient. But she wouldn't be a patient after she left the hospital.

Polly smiled to herself. Here she went again, trying to match people up. Because she'd been so happy in her marriage. And she wanted the same thing for other young couples.

A voice broke into her thoughts. It was Cynthia Price, one of the other nurses on the floor.

"I couldn't help overhearing you and the doctor talking. Are you really taking that Jane Doe woman home with you?" Price asked. She was a slender brunette in her mid-thirties, and as far as Polly could tell, she had the right nursing skills, but she didn't have much empathy for the patients.

"Yes."

Polly's colleague fiddled with the ballpoint pen she was holding. "I don't like to interfere, but isn't that taking a chance?"

"What do you mean?"

"She could be…" The woman raised a shoulder. "She could be a thief or Lord knows what."

"I think I'm a good judge of character, and I don't believe she's a thief or a murderer. But Dr. Delano and I both have the idea she's in some kind of trouble."

"Yes, I heard you discussing it. What do you think it is?"

"When she gets her memory back, we'll know." Polly paused for a second. "I think it would be better if you don't tell anyone she left with me."

Cynthia considered the request. "What if her family comes looking for her or something? What if they're worried sick about her?"

Polly thought for a moment. "Don't tell anyone where she's gone, but get their name and number and call me."

"You sound like a character in a spy novel."

Polly laughed. "I'm being cautious is all."

The conversation was interrupted when she saw Elizabeth look out of her room toward the nurses' station.

"Here she comes now." As Elizabeth focused on them, Polly said, "Thanks for your help," wondering if she could rely on Cynthia's discretion.

ELIZABETH LOOKED INTO the hall. Once again she'd been hoping to see Dr. Delano. He wasn't there, and she was annoyed with herself for fixating on him and feeling disappointed. But that was logical, she told herself. He'd been the only link to her past. Deliberately she ordered herself not to dwell on the rest of it.

Polly Kramer smiled as Elizabeth came down the hall, then asked, "How are you feeling?"

"Physically, okay."

"Good. Let's leave."

"Mrs. Kramer…"

"Please call me Polly."

"Polly, I appreciate what you're doing for me."

"I wouldn't do it if I didn't feel good about it myself."

Polly helped her into a wheelchair and then into the elevator where, she gave Elizabeth a studied glance. "You look very professional in that outfit."

"I was thinking the same thing. I'm very buttoned up."

"You obviously have a job that requires a polished appearance."

"The shoes are a little dowdy."

"They're practical."

"What do you think I do for a living?"

"You could be a lawyer."

Elizabeth contemplated the answer. "Perhaps."

"What do *you* think?"

"A teacher would be closer, but that doesn't quite work for me, either."

As they exited the elevator and Polly wheeled the chair out the staff-only door, she said, "Your outfit gives you the look of authority, but it isn't exactly comfortable for relaxing. I was thinking we could stop at a discount department store, and you could pick up a few things."

Elizabeth felt her chest tighten. A line from a play leaped into her head. Something about relying on the kindnesses of strangers. "I don't have any cash, and I'm already imposing on you by staying at your house."

"Nonsense. I'll be right back." The nurse got her vehicle and drove to the curb, where Elizabeth got in.

"I hate the idea of your spending any money on me," she said when she was settled.

Polly made a tsking sound. "I'd feel like I was abandoning you if I just left you twisting in the wind."

"Do you take in stray dogs and cats, too?"

Her companion laughed. "No. I'm more people oriented."

They stopped at the automatic gate where Polly inserted her card, then drove out of the hospital parking lot.

"Does any of this look familiar?" she asked.

"I'm not seeing anything that jumps out at me," Elizabeth answered.

"Well, let's try something more specific." A few minutes later, she pulled into a suburban shopping center and led Elizabeth inside the discount store, where they picked up a cart. "I thought we'd try the drugstore section. Why don't you walk around and see if you can spot products that seem familiar?"

Elizabeth gave her a grateful look. "That's a fantastic idea. Thanks." She grabbed her own cart and began wheeling it up and down aisles until she spotted a brand of makeup that she thought she might have used. Also shampoo and deodorant.

"We need to keep track of what I spend, so I can pay you back," she said again.

"If that makes you feel more comfortable."

"Of course it does."

Elizabeth chose a lipstick and some moisturizer, as well. "Did it look like I had on much makeup when I came in?" she asked.

"Maybe a little eye shadow."

She selected a packet that had a couple shades of gray. "Fifty shades," she muttered.

"What?"

"Isn't there a famous book called *Fifty Shades of Grey?*"

Mrs. Kramer laughed. "More like infamous than famous."

"Why?"

The older woman flushed. "I believe it's some kind of sex thing."

"Oh. I guess I didn't read it."

"Neither did I. I'm just repeating what I heard." Polly changed the subject quickly. "Let's go look at the casual clothing."

Elizabeth might have protested about spending more money on herself, but she wasn't going to be borrowing any of the other woman's shorter and wider clothing.

Maybe Polly was following her thoughts because she said, "I have some big old T-shirts you could use to sleep in."

"Good. One less thing I need to worry about," she answered, thinking that this was certainly a surreal experience—although it didn't quite come up to the standard of touching Matthew Delano and getting into his mind. Or the other part—the sexual part.

Trying to put *that* out of her thoughts, she hurried to the ladies' department, where she found shelves full of inexpensive T-shirts. She selected three—deep blue, turquoise and purple.

"Perfect for your hair and skin tone," Mrs. Kramer approved.

"I guess I know my colors."

She shuffled through the piles and pulled out size eights,

which turned out to fit her well, along with a pair of jeans and a three-pack of panties, figuring she could wash them every other day. And the bra she had on would be fine.

"Get some socks and tennis shoes," her guardian angel advised.

Again she felt her stomach clench at the idea of spending someone else's money so freely, but she couldn't think of an alternative.

On the groceries side of the store, Polly asked, "What do you want to eat?"

Another memory test. "Will you let me do the cooking?"

"If you're not too tired."

She selected a package of ground beef, canned kidney beans and salsa, pleased that she could come up with a set of ingredients that made sense. "Do you have onions, chili powder and cumin?"

"I believe I do."

"Then I'll make us chili."

"Do you need a recipe?"

She thought about what would be involved in making the dish. "No, I can do it."

"You like to cook?"

"I think so."

"One more thing you know," Mrs. Kramer said.

Elizabeth nodded. It was like playing a game where she didn't quite know the rules. But some of them came back to her—basically what she considered ordinary things. Or general things. The part that dealt specifically with her own life remained a mystery.

As they drove to Polly Kramer's house, Elizabeth kept looking behind her.

"Is something wrong, dear?" the older woman asked.

"I can't shake the idea that somebody is following me."

"Do you see anyone you recognize?"

She sighed. "No. I'm just nervous about it." She didn't

want to say why. That, when she'd touched Matthew Delano, she had had a memory of someone following her and that trying to get away had caused her automobile accident.

They pulled into Polly Kramer's driveway.

She lived in a redbrick rancher in a close-in suburb, probably built in the 1950s, Elizabeth thought, wondering how she'd placed it in time. There was a low chain-link fence around a half-acre yard and a carport instead of a garage.

"My husband and I bought this house forty years ago," Polly said as they pulled into the driveway.

"Is he home?" Elizabeth asked, looking around for another car.

"He died a few years ago."

"I'm sorry."

"It's one of the reasons I'd love to have some company. The house isn't all that big, but sometimes I feel like I'm rattling around inside."

"I understand," Elizabeth said automatically. Because of personal knowledge of loss? she wondered. Or because she was good at getting in touch with people's emotions? Which would be strange if she basically felt disconnected from everybody.

"Dan was an engineer. He made a good living and had a nice pension, and I still collect most of it. Plus we paid off the mortgage years ago. I don't really have to work at the hospital, but I like the contact with people. So don't worry about my paying for a few things you need. We'll get it sorted out later."

"Thank you," Elizabeth answered, overwhelmed by the kindness of this woman she barely knew. Was Elizabeth the type of person who would do the same thing for a stranger? And was that how she'd gotten in trouble? The question stopped her, and she thought she caught the edge of a memory, but she wasn't able to pull it into her mind.

"You come in and get settled," Polly was saying. "You

probably want to rest awhile, and there's no need to start dinner for a couple hours."

Elizabeth nodded. In fact, the brief shopping trip had taken a lot out of her.

Polly showed her through a living room, furnished in a comfortable contemporary style, to a pleasant bedroom in the back of the house. "I keep the sheets fresh," she said. "Go on and lie down for a bit."

"You're sure you don't need help putting the groceries away?"

"We only got a few things. You just relax."

"Thank you." Elizabeth took off her slacks, jacket and shoes, and laid down, thinking she'd get up in a few minutes.

MATTHEW DELANO COULDN'T shake the feeling of guilt that hung over him as he finished making his rounds, then went down to his office on the first floor, where he entered some information into the computerized patients' charts. On Tuesdays and Thursdays he saw patients in the hospital clinic, but he had the afternoon free today. And he couldn't stop thinking about Elizabeth Doe.

She was in trouble, and he'd walked away from her because he was uncomfortable with the sexual heat that had flared between them when he had touched her. But he felt like a bastard for abandoning her when she wasn't in any kind of shape to fend for herself.

He told himself ethics cut both ways. What if something terrible happened to her that he could have prevented by helping her bring back the memories she needed?

He was silently debating what to do when a knock on his office door interrupted him.

"Come in," he called.

A man wearing dark slacks and a navy blazer over a white dress shirt stepped into Matt's office. The stranger looked to be in his late twenties, and he had broad shoulders, a muscular build and large dangerous-looking hands. His face wasn't particularly remarkable, although perhaps he had broken his nose sometime in the past.

The overall impression he gave was negative, although Matt couldn't exactly explain why. Just as he'd gotten the feeling that Elizabeth Doe was a good person, he sensed that this guy was "bad." There was something behind his eyes that told Matt his mood could turn deadly in an instant.

"Dr. Delano?"

"Yes," he said, still sizing up the man.

"I'm Bob Wilson. I understand you saw a patient with amnesia?"

"I'm not at liberty to discuss my patients."

"Yes, of course. I understand completely. But I think she might be my sister."

"Why?"

"She told me that she was coming over yesterday, but she never showed up."

"And you haven't heard from her?"

"No."

"The woman I treated was listed as Jane Doe. What's your sister's name?"

"Elizabeth Simmons."

He hoped he didn't show any reaction. The Elizabeth part was right, but was that really her last name? And why did he doubt this guy? "Do you have her picture?"

"Of course." The man opened his wallet and took out a photograph that looked like it might have been taken for a college yearbook.

"Yes, that's her," he reluctantly said. There was no way out of the admission because, if he lied about it, it was easily exposed since his having treated her was a matter of record.

Wilson's face lit up, but not in a way Matt liked.

"Thank God. Do you know where she's gone?"

This lie was easy. "Sorry."

"You're sure you have no idea?"

"Sorry," he said again. "I can't help you. I'd left the floor before she was discharged."

The man's expression turned hard. "If you do hear about her, I'd like you to call me." He took out a business card that read Bob Wilson and handed it over. There was a phone number on the card but nothing else besides the name.

"What do you do, Mr. Wilson?"

"I'm in sales."

"Why don't you have that on your card?"

"I'm between jobs."

Matt wanted to ask, "Then why have a card?" but he kept the question to himself.

Wilson gave Matt a penetrating look, and Matt had the feeling that he wanted to say, "You're in big trouble if you don't call."

But he said nothing more.

THE RINGING OF THE phone woke Elizabeth, and when she looked outside, it was getting dark.

She dressed in her new clothes, then hurried into the living room, hoping it might be Matthew Delano on the phone. But it sounded like Polly was talking to someone else. She had a pad of paper and a pencil in her hand and was writing something down.

When she hung up, she looked at Elizabeth. "A man came to the nursing station asking about you."

"Who?"

"He said his name was Bob Wilson and that he was your brother."

"Bob Wilson," she repeated, saying the name a couple of times aloud.

"Does that mean anything to you?"

"No, but that's not surprising. I mean, nothing has come back to me except—" She stopped abruptly.

"Except what?"

"Except the part about my name," she said, unwilling to relate that, when Matthew Delano had touched her, a whole slew of memories had come flashing back to her. But telling Polly about that would sound strange. Really, Elizabeth wouldn't have believed it herself if it hadn't happened to her.

And she didn't want to make her benefactor think that Elizabeth Doe had lost her marbles as well as her memory. "This Bob Wilson person spoke to someone at the hospital?" she asked.

"Yes."

"Who?"

"Cynthia Price. She's one of the other nurses on the floor. She heard me and Dr. Delano talking about my taking you home."

Elizabeth felt her stomach knot. "But she didn't tell him where I'd gone?"

"No."

"Why not?"

"I asked her not to."

"Why?"

"Because Dr. Delano and I both agreed that you're in some kind of trouble, and it's best to find out what it is before revealing your location."

"Thank you," she breathed, a feeling of relief settling over her.

In the next second, it popped into her head that the normal thing to do in this situation would be to call the police, but she dismissed that idea as soon as it surfaced. It simply didn't feel right. Which was a hunch she didn't much like.

She folded her arms across her chest and rubbed her upper arms.

"You look worried," Polly said.

"I can't help wondering if Cynthia told him where I was."

"I understand, but she's very reliable. Why don't you start dinner? I've got something I need to take care of."

"If you'll show me around your kitchen first."

Polly led her to the back of the house, where she gave her a quick tour and got out some of the supplies that Elizabeth was going to need, including a big pot.

"You know how to use an electric stove?"

"You have to wait a moment for the heat to go up or down."

"That's right. Will you be okay for a while?" Polly asked.

"I think so."

Mrs. Kramer left, and Elizabeth put the pot on the stove, then used the knife and cutting board to chop the onions.

She put them into the pot with the ground beef and began to sauté them, soothed by the simple act of meal preparation. It was familiar, routine work, but it was also reassuring doing something useful and comforting that she had no problem remembering how to do.

When the meat began to stick to the bottom of the pot, she turned down the heat and added a little water, stirring as she watched it change from red to brown.

Should she add the spices while the meat and onions were browning or wait until she got the salsa into the pot?

She let the task of cooking dinner completely absorb her, breathing in the smell of the chili when she had all the ingredients in the pot, including a can of tomato sauce she found in the pantry because she needed to supplement the salsa. She was just tasting the seasonings when the doorbell rang.

Elizabeth went rigid, then glanced toward the back door. That guy who'd come to the hospital had found out where she was, and she had to get away before he came in here.

Chapter Four

When Polly opened the front door, Matt stepped into the living room. "Thanks for calling me."

"I didn't mean to drag you over, but thanks for coming," the nurse said.

"I was telling myself it was unethical to keep seeing Elizabeth. Now I think it's unethical not to, if I think she's in trouble."

Mrs. Kramer nodded. "That makes sense."

"Where is she?"

"In the kitchen. Cooking dinner. I thought it would give her something to do."

Matt took an appreciative sniff. "Smells good. Did you have to help her, or did she remember how to fix a meal?"

"I just showed her around the kitchen, and she got busy all by herself."

"Good."

They walked to the back of the house and stopped short when they saw the kitchen was empty, a simmering pot was on the stove, and the back door was open.

"Where is she?" Matt asked, feeling his stomach knot.

"She was right here," Polly murmured.

Matt looked toward the open back door and cursed under his breath. "Did you say something that would frighten her?"

"I told her a man who called himself Bob Wilson had been asking for her at the nurses' station. That was before

I called you, and you said the same guy had been to your office."

Matt clenched his fists as he walked to the back door and looked out at the darkened yard. "She must have heard the doorbell, assumed the worst and ran. You look through the house in case she changed her mind and ducked back inside. I'll look outside."

"I'm sorry. I should have warned her that you were coming over," Polly said.

"We'll find her," he said, to reassure himself and Mrs. Kramer. As he stepped onto the cracked patio, a security light came on.

"Elizabeth. Elizabeth, it's me. Matt Delano," he called.

When she didn't answer, he looked around. Polly's yard butted against the property in back of her and to the sides. Elizabeth would have to climb over several fences to get far. His gaze landed on the metal storage shed just inside the range of the security light.

Quickly he hurried to the door and thrust it open, although he didn't charge inside, because his experiences in Africa had taught him not to rush into an enclosed space if he didn't know who might be in there. Lucky for him. He jumped back as a baseball bat came swooshing down. It missed his head by less than an inch.

The woman holding the weapon stared at him. "Oh, Lord, Matthew. I'm so sorry."

"It's okay. Polly told you someone called the nurses' station, right?"

"Yes."

"I think the same guy came to my office after he tried to get information from the staff. He said you were Elizabeth Simmons."

"That doesn't sound right. I mean the last name."

"Why not?"

She shrugged, looking so lost and helpless that his heart

turned over. But she wasn't exactly helpless. Instinct had told her to run when she'd heard the doorbell ring. And she'd been prepared to defend herself.

He had vowed not to touch her again, yet the desperate look on her face drew him forward. Unable to stop himself, he reached for her, pulling her into his arms, holding her close as he stepped into the shed.

"She's not inside. Did you find her?" Polly's voice called from behind him.

"Yes. She's fine. She's in here. We'll be right there," he managed to say, amazed that he sounded so rational when his brain and his senses were already on overload.

He said they were coming back, but he didn't move, only absorbed the reality of Elizabeth's body molded against his.

He had been trying to stay away from her. Now he knew that was an impossible goal. Not when they already meant more to each other than anyone had ever meant to either one of them. It was a crazy evaluation. How could two people who had just met mean *everything* to each other? But he knew it was true as he wrapped her more tightly in his arms.

In the hospital he'd barely touched her—just his hand on her arm at first—and the memories had come. Then holding her closer had been enough to trigger additional memories and so much more. Now they were alone in a dark, private space where it was impossible to pull away from each other. At least that was the way it felt.

Her own arms came up and locked around his waist, holding him close, and he was lost to everything except the woman in his arms. Her sweet scent, the feel of her silky skin, the crush of her body against his.

The same thing happened as before. Memories flooded through him. Her memories. And he knew she was picking up things from him—things that he had tried hard to forget. He was traveling through the backcountry, and he had come to a village that looked deserted. But the smell rising from the huts told him a different story.

He forced himself to look in one, seeing the mangled bodies of a mother, a father and three children piled on the floor. He backed out, retching, unable to understand why anyone had felt compelled to slaughter innocent civilians who were just trying to live their lives as best they could. Had the rebels done it or the government? He didn't even know.

He thrust away the horrible images and slammed into one of Elizabeth's memories. An early recollection that had always torn at her. She was in an elementary-school classroom. He saw bright pictures on the wall, pictures painted by the students. And words that might be the spelling lesson for the week.

She was sitting in a chair, watching as other children leaped up and ran to their parents. It must be some sort of special school day, and everyone was hugging and interacting. But Elizabeth sat in her seat, and her mother was standing near the door. Finally Elizabeth got up and ran to the woman, the way the other children had done. But it wasn't the same. Elizabeth knew it wasn't the same, and so did her mother. They were separated in ways that Elizabeth didn't understand. She wanted desperately to bridge that gap, but she didn't know how.

The scene was an echo of his own memories. His parents had been well-off. They'd wanted the best for their son— and they'd given Matt everything they could. Even love. And Matt had tried to respond, but he simply couldn't give them what they craved from him. What he craved, if he were honest about it.

And now he suddenly had what he had always been searching for, from a woman who was a stranger.

In her memory, he saw another scene. She was an adult now, bending over a bed, comforting a young and beautiful Asian woman who turned her head away and wouldn't look her in the eye.

All of the memories—his and hers—made him sad. It was much more gratifying to focus on the here and now—on the woman he held in his arms.

His head had started to pound, but he ignored the pain as he moved farther back into the shed, taking her with him. The door was at an angle that made it close behind them, shutting them inside. In the dark, they clung to each other for support and a whole lot of other reasons.

He hadn't admitted it, but he had needed so much more from her since the first moment he had touched her. Now, here, he couldn't resist the pull. Unable to stop himself, he lowered his mouth to hers for a kiss that was almost frantic. His lips moved over hers, and he smiled when he realized she'd been tasting the dish she was cooking on the stove.

But he stopped thinking about the chili as he stroked his hands up and down her back. Seeking more, he lifted the hem of the T-shirt she was wearing and slipped his hands underneath, flattening them against her warm skin, loving the feel of her and the contact that was so much more than he could put into words.

He knew he was arousing her, just as she knew she was arousing him. Holding her, kissing her, touching her was so very sexual, even with the underlying layers of memories from her past and his.

He'd made love with women before, looking for something that he was sure he wasn't going to find. Sex had always been physically satisfying, but there had invariably been something missing, the same disappointment that had dogged his life.

Again he knew it was like that for her. Searching and never finding. Until now.

I didn't go out and sleep with a bunch of guys.

I know. I was just thinking how it was the same for you. Disappointing.

The exchange stunned him. Neither of them had spoken aloud, yet he'd clearly heard her respond to his thought. And he had responded to hers.

That was enough of a shock to make him drop his hands and step back. What was he doing? What were they doing?

And he was glad he had broken the contact when the door of the shed opened. Whirling, he found himself staring at Polly Kramer.

"Oh, I'm sorry."

"No. We were just coming back to the house," Matt managed to say, hearing the thick quality of his own voice and not quite able to meet the older woman's eyes.

"Are you all right?" Polly asked Elizabeth.

Elizabeth ran a hand through her hair. "Yes."

Polly turned back to the house, and Matt waited a beat before asking Elizabeth, "Does your head hurt?"

"Yes. What do you think that means, Doctor?"

He laughed. "I can speculate, but I don't know."

By mutual agreement, he turned and walked out of the shed, and she followed. He didn't have to see her to know she was walking behind him.

He wanted to talk about what had happened between them. The sexual pull. The memories. And something even more startling. Actual words exchanged in their heads.

"You heard what I said?" he asked.

"Yes."

There was no need to explain he was talking about the silent exchange.

"I turned the chili down," Mrs. Kramer said when they stepped into the kitchen.

"Thank you," Elizabeth answered. She went straight to the pot, stirred it and tasted.

"How is it?" Matt asked, his voice still sounding not quite normal.

"Good."

"We should eat," Mrs. Kramer said. "You two sit down, and I'll serve."

"I can get us all a glass of water," Matt said, thinking it was a lame comment. But everything felt stilted now except the intimacy of being with Elizabeth.

"We can serve ourselves from the stove," Mrs. Kramer said.

They all did, then sat at the table, which would be a perfectly normal thing to do, except that nothing would ever be normal again.

That was a pretty exaggerated way to put it, but Matt knew it was true.

"Where are you from?" Elizabeth asked him, startling him by breaking into his overblown thoughts.

He struggled to deal with the question. "New Orleans."

"What did your parents do?"

"My dad was an oil company executive. My mom sort of did the country-club thing. They live in Santa Barbara, California, now."

"Were you an only child?"

"Yes," he answered, thinking that his mother had told him she'd had a lot of trouble getting pregnant. She'd been torn between wanting another child and not wanting to go through the rigors of a fertility clinic again. Although that had been her decision, she'd made it clear that he hadn't been the loving son she'd wanted. But he didn't tell the women he dated any of that.

"Did you grow up down there?"

"Yes."

Elizabeth was staring off into space.

"What?" he asked.

"New Orleans."

"What about it?"

"I remember stuff about the city. I mean I can picture... Jackson Square," she said.

"You've probably seen pictures."

"I think I've been there. And the French Market."

"Okay."

He waited for her to give him more information, but she only shook her head. "Maybe I'm wrong."

"We'll assume you're right."

"If it's true, it gives us something in common."

He nodded, wondering if it was important, and why it might be.

"Do you know how to cook *pain perdu?*" he asked.

"French toast?"

"Yeah."

"That's easy."

"What about gumbo?"

"I have a general idea of what's in it, but I'd have to look up a recipe if I wanted to make some."

"Most people would, I think." He looked at Elizabeth. "Where are you from?"

The answer to the question lurked below the surface of her mind. "Nice try," she murmured.

"I thought I'd give it a shot."

They were all silent for several moments while they ate.

"Well, this chili is delicious," Mrs. Kramer said, as she spooned up more of the beans and beef mixture.

"Thank you," Elizabeth answered.

Again they resumed eating, and Mrs. Kramer broke the silence once more as they finished the meal. "How did you get so far north?" she asked Matt.

"I went to medical school at Hopkins. After..." He stopped and glanced at Elizabeth. "After Africa, I decided Baltimore was as good a place as any to practice medicine."

"You intend to settle down here?" Mrs. Kramer asked.

He involuntarily glanced at Elizabeth again, thinking that everything they said had a double meaning or a subcontext that only the two of them could really follow.

"I...don't know." He cleared his throat, changing the subject abruptly as he looked at Elizabeth. "Do you want to try hypnosis?"

"What?"

"With many people, it can help recover memories."

"You mean now?"

"After we finish eating."

"You know how to do it?"

"I had a class," he said. "We could try it."

Elizabeth gave that some consideration. "Okay. What do you want me to do?"

"Just sit in a chair and relax."

"I can clean up," Polly said.

"You shouldn't have to," Elizabeth protested. "You already have a houseguest."

"You cooked us a delicious meal. I'll do the cleaning. That's only fair."

Matt and Elizabeth got up, carefully avoiding touching each other. They went into the living room where she glanced around, then settled into an overstuffed chair, looking apprehensive.

"What should I do?"

"Like I said, get comfortable."

"That's difficult."

For a whole lot of reasons, some of them having to do with her situation and some with him, he knew.

He sat down on the sofa, trying to relax and not having perfect success.

"Lean back. Look up at the line where the wall meets the ceiling."

"Why?"

"It puts your eyes at the right level."

She did as he said, and he kept speaking to her in a soothing voice. "Relax now. Relax now. Relax now."

He saw some of the tension drain out of her features.

"How do you feel?"

"Good."

"There's nothing to worry about. We're just going to see if we can bring back more of your past."

"Yes," she murmured.

"And when I tell you to wake up, you will. Do you understand?"

"Yes."

"We can start with a little mental vacation. Let's go somewhere where you'd like to be."

She thought about that. "I'm not sure."

"Most people like the beach. Does that work for you?"

She waited a beat before answering, "Yes."

"We're at the beach. You're on a chaise, lying in the sun. It feels good on your face and body. The waves are rolling up across the sand."

"Um."

"Let's go a little deeper into relaxation. You go back to the resort where you're staying. You go inside, and there's a flight of steps. You go down, one step at a time."

"Okay."

"Every step takes you deeper into relaxation." He could see from her face that it was working.

"What's at the bottom of the stairs?" he asked.

Her body jerked.

"What?"

"Women. They're frightened."

"Why?"

"They're a long way from home." Her body jerked again. "I don't want to be there."

"Okay."

Her eyes blinked open, focusing on him.

She looked so lost and alone that every instinct urged him to cross the room and take her in his arms again, but he knew that wasn't such a great idea, given what happened every time they touched.

"Yes," she murmured.

"You know what I'm thinking?"

"It's all over your face."

"Sorry I'm so transparent."

"Not to most people, I think."

"I want to ask about that memory."

She shuddered. "It's nothing good."

"Is it something recent?"

Her vision turned inward. "I think so."

"But you aren't sure?"

"I'm betting it has to do with that man who was following me. Maybe I saw something I wasn't supposed to. And the mob is after me."

"The mob?"

"You have a better explanation?"

"I wish I knew, but the part about your stumbling into something sounds right." He thought for a moment. "What kind of women?"

"Young and pretty."

"What race?"

"Why are you asking?"

"You had a memory of an Asian woman before."

"These were Caucasian."

"Okay. Do you think it has anything to do with your job?"

"Good question." She shook her head. "Maybe it would help to try word association."

"I think we shouldn't try to push this any further tonight. You've had a tiring day—coming off a mild concussion."

"Yes, probably pushing to come up with any more answers right now is a waste of time."

"I don't want to leave you and Mrs. Kramer alone, with that Wilson guy out there."

"I think we'll be all right."

"But you took off out the back when the doorbell rang."

She shook her head. "Yeah. I'm jumpy, but that doesn't mean it's logical."

He wrote down his cell phone number and set it on the coffee table. "Call me if anything worries you. Or if you have any memories."

"I think the latter's more likely when you're around."

He nodded, looking at her hand. It was so tempting to reach out and touch her. They'd get memories, all right. And a lot more.

She looked up at him and away, and it was obvious again that she knew what he was thinking.

"I'll tell Mrs. Kramer I'm leaving."

Elizabeth was still in the living room when he returned, and he had to force himself not to stop and touch her. And force himself to leave, for that matter. He'd forged a connection with this woman who didn't even know her name, and he wanted to strengthen that connection. But nothing had changed as far as his ethics were concerned. He still had no business coming on to her.

Chapter Five

Matthew had been right. Elizabeth was exhausted. She dropped off again almost as soon as she crawled into bed. For a few hours, she was able to sleep. But sometime in the small hours of the morning, a dream grabbed her.

She was on her way to work. And a car was behind her, inching up. There were men in the car, and she knew they wanted to hurt her. Because…

Her hands clenched on the steering wheel as she struggled to grab on to the answer. The only thing she could remember was "the women."

She'd been trying to help the women. She had to remember that. It was an important clue. But there was no time for clues right now. She had to get away because the men were going to kill her if they caught up. She wasn't sure why she thought so. But she knew it was true. Well, they were going to question her first, because they wanted to know how she had found out about the women.

She pressed on the accelerator, desperate to escape, weaving down an alley before shooting out onto the street. A truck was in the way, and she slammed into a lamppost.

This time, she woke with a muffled scream, wondering where she was.

Then it came back to her. At least the past day. She glanced at the clock. It was four in the morning, and she knew where she was—at Polly Kramer's house, the nice woman on the hospital nursing staff who had brought Elizabeth to her home, a woman who couldn't even remember her name.

At least she knew her first name. *Elizabeth.* She'd gotten that when she had touched Matt Delano the first time. Something happened whenever they touched. A flood of memories—his and hers. Was she fixated on him because she couldn't remember anything else about herself?

It was an interesting theory, but she knew it wasn't true. Whatever had transpired between them was real—and unique. The exchange of information and the startling sexual awareness that pulled them together every time they touched. And then the speaking to each other, mind to mind. She shouldn't forget about that.

She squeezed her hands into fists. He could help her, but that sexual connection was keeping him away because of his strict code of morality.

Movement at the door made her tense and glance up. Polly Kramer was standing there, staring at her.

Elizabeth relaxed when she saw who it was.

"Are you all right, dear?"

"Yes. I had a nightmare. I'm sorry I woke you."

"I'm a very light sleeper. Are you okay?"

"Yes," she lied.

"Was the nightmare a memory?"

"Maybe." She related the dream.

Polly lingered for a few more moments. "And that's all you remember?"

"Yes," she answered, again making the decision not to tell her about what else Matt had pulled from her mind.

When Polly had gone back to bed, Elizabeth lay in the dark, thinking about the broken recollections—trying to force herself past the blank wall before the car chase.

What had she been doing when she got herself into trouble?

Matthew had said all hypnosis was self-hypnosis. Did that mean she could try to do what he'd guided her through before?

She considered the idea, then rejected it. What if she couldn't wake up and nobody was here to pull her back?

She made a frustrated sound. Every which way she turned led to some new dead end. No, not really new. Just another manifestation of the same old sense of defeat.

She tried to go back to sleep, but that was beyond her. Finally she heaved herself up and went down the hall. Hoping she wasn't going to wake up Polly, she prowled around the kitchen, checking ingredients in the refrigerator and the pantry. Polly had the makings of a vegetarian minestrone soup. Well, vegetarian except for the chicken broth.

Yes, she could make that and put it in the refrigerator for later.

She stopped and laughed out loud. Was cooking what she did to relax herself?

She didn't know, but it was something to occupy her mind while she tried to get the rest of her life back.

CYNTHIA PRICE WAS back at the nurses' station in the morning when another young man showed up. Last time it had been a guy who had said he was Elizabeth's brother, although Cynthia had wondered if it was true. This time it was a different story.

"I understand you had a woman here who doesn't remember her name or anything else," he began.

"Yes," Cynthia answered cautiously.

"She didn't have any identification on her?"

"No purse."

"She was in an auto accident. Did the police check the car's registration?"

"That was a dead end. The car belonged to someone else who's on an extended trip outside the country."

"Your patient's a mystery woman."

"Uh-huh."

"I was thinking I might be able to help her."

"Who are you?"

"Oh, sorry. I'm a newspaper reporter with the *Baltimore Observer*."

"Never heard of it."

"We're an online publication. That gives us the flexibility to get the news up quickly."

Cynthia waited for him to say more.

"If I did an article about the woman—Jane Doe—someone might come forward to, you know, claim her."

"We don't have a picture of her."

"But do you know where she went?"

Cynthia hesitated, weighing the upside and the downside. Polly had said not to talk about Elizabeth, but this was a newspaper reporter who might be able to help her.

"She went home with one of our nurses," she finally said.

"One of the nurses from this floor."

Cynthia swallowed. "Yes, but if you get someone who thinks they know her, you can call me, and I'll contact her."

"You can't give me her name?"

"I'd rather not."

"Okay. And what else can you tell me? Can you give me a description of her?"

Cynthia thought for a moment. "She was in her late twenties or early thirties. Her hair was short and dark, curly. Her eyes were blue. Her face was oval-shaped. She's about five feet five inches tall and weighs about 110 pounds. Does that help?"

"That's excellent."

Cynthia was starting to wonder if she had done the right thing. "What did you say your name was?"

"Jack Regan."

"You have a card?"

He handed her one with his name and a phone number.
She bent it back and forth in her hand.

"I'll call if I get a lead," he said.

"When will the article be out?"

"I'll let you know."

The man left, and Cynthia looked toward the phone.
Should she call Polly? Or should she just act like nothing
had happened? In the end she didn't make the call.

ELIZABETH WAS THINKING that she would have never in her
life have considered finding herself in this helpless situation.
Then she laughed because she was making up the "never in
her life" part. The truth was that if she had imagined this,
she didn't know about it because the memory was missing.

She showered and dressed, and spent a restless morning
flipping through TV channels.

Over two hundred channels and nothing held her interest.
As she looked out the back window, her gaze roamed over
Polly's weedy garden. If Elizabeth went out and worked in
it for a few hours, at least she'd be doing something con-
structive.

This was one of the days Polly didn't go to work. At least
that's what she'd told Elizabeth, who hoped the nurse hadn't
made special arrangements to stay home and watch over her.

SO FAR SO GOOD, Derek Lang decided. Hank Patterson, who
had posed as Jack Regan, returned with valuable information.

"Elizabeth Forester is staying with a nurse who was on
duty yesterday."

Derek swung to his computer and consulted one of the
many databases he had access to.

He quickly came up with the personnel files of Memorial Hospital and found out who was on the nursing staff.
Next he used a hacker program to get into the hospital work

schedules and was able to zero in on the medical unit that had treated Forester.

A few moments later, he looked up from the computer. "There were three nurses on duty in her area. We know it's not the Price woman. That leaves two others." He gave Patterson the names. "You and Southwell check them out."

When Patterson had gone, Derek went back to the computer. It might be good to know what doctors had been on duty, too.

ELIZABETH FOUND POLLY folding laundry in the bedroom.

"I'm going to be out back, doing some yard work."

"You don't have to do anything like that."

"I want to."

"All right, dear."

"Do you have some gardening gloves?"

"In the shed."

Elizabeth took a plastic grocery bag from the kitchen. She could stuff weeds inside it and then periodically empty the bag at the side of the shed. And then she could ask Polly what she wanted done with the mess.

She slipped out the back and stood on the cracked concrete patio for a moment before crossing to the shed. As soon as she stepped inside, she started thinking about what she and Matthew had been doing in here last night.

Banishing that intimate scene from her mind, she located the gloves, exited the shed and looked around. The garden had been laid out with several flower beds, although it seemed that Polly had lost interest in keeping the place up. But really, it could look much better. Elizabeth crossed to the far right corner, got down on her knees and began pulling at the various weeds that had taken over. She didn't know the names of them, but she knew which were the plants that were choking out the flowers.

She'd been working for a half hour when the back door

opened. Expecting to see Polly, she looked up. Instead of the nurse, a man was standing in the doorway staring at her. A man with a gun that had a strangely long barrel.

She gasped.

He gave her a smile that didn't reach his eyes. "Let's go."

"No."

"You want me to shoot you here?" he asked.

She raised her chin. "You won't. You want information from me."

His face registered surprise and annoyance. "Yeah, but what if I shoot you in the kneecap?"

"Are you going to risk it?"

Chapter Six

Elizabeth was shocked at her own audacity, yet in the back of her mind, she had been expecting something like this all along. Men had been chasing her, and she'd been sure they were looking for her. Now she wasn't really surprised that one of them had caught up with her. They'd been desperate to find her, and it had been bound to happen.

A horrible thought struck her. The man had come through the house, and Polly had been in there. Had she hidden from him, or had he found her? And what had he done to her?

She clenched her teeth, holding back the questions. Perhaps he hadn't seen Polly and she'd gotten to the phone to call 9-1-1.

Stalling for time, she said, "What if I still don't know who I am?"

"We'll find out if you're telling the truth."

The light behind the man changed, and she saw another figure standing there. Was it the other man who'd been chasing her in the car? Then he shifted to the right, and she saw it was Matthew Delano.

Her heart leaped—with relief and fear. Matthew had arrived, but what good was that going to do either one of them against a man with a gun?

She tried not to look directly at Matt, tried not to give away that there was anyone behind the man.

Matt was staring at her with intense concentration on his

face, and she realized with a zing of recognition that he was trying to tell her something.

Mind to mind. They'd done that once before, when they were touching. Now he was ten feet away and struggling to send her a message.

She strained to understand what he was trying to tell her. It was fuzzy. Half-formed, like a radio transmission full of static. She struggled to focus on the words while she kept her gaze on the man with the gun. And finally a message solidified in her head.

If you hear me, raise your shoulder. Then drop to the ground.

As soon as she got the message, she did as he said, raising her shoulder, then dropping down, out of the line of fire.

"Wha…"

That was all the man said before Matt was on him, throwing him down where he stood.

The gun went off, a silenced sound as the guy fell. She dashed forward and lashed out with her foot, kicking him in the face. He screamed, and Matt grabbed his hair, lifting his head and smashing it against the concrete patio.

The man went still, and Matt heaved himself up.

She turned to him. "What are you doing here?"

"I tried to stay away, but I couldn't. Come on, we have to get going."

"Where's Polly?"

Matt's expression turned grim. "I'm sorry. She's dead."

Elizabeth felt her chest go tight, hardly able to process the words. "Dead?"

"Yeah." He paused for a moment before saying, "He shot her. Used a silencer so you wouldn't hear it."

She moaned. "But…"

"I know. It's awful, but we have to get out of here."

"Where are we going?"

"I don't know. Away."

He grabbed her hand, and she felt the familiar jolt of sexual awareness. Struggling to ignore it, she let him lead her into the house, but she stopped short when she saw blood trailing out of the laundry room. Following it, she found Polly lying in a crumpled heap in the door to the laundry room, a pool of blood under her.

"We were just talking about garden gloves," she whispered.

"I'm sorry," was all he could offer.

The reality of everything that had happened in the past few minutes jolted her. "Did she fight him?"

"I can't tell."

He turned toward the wall phone, picked up the receiver and punched in 9-1-1.

"What is the nature of your emergency?"

"There's been a murder at 2520 Wandering Way," he said, giving Polly's address.

"Stay on the line and…"

He hung up. "We can't stay around."

"But…"

"We have to be out of here when the cops get here," he said with conviction. Picking up a dish towel, he wiped off the phone. "You bought some clothes. Where are they?"

"Bedroom."

He strode down a short hall and came back with the bag from the discount store. "Let's go."

When she couldn't manage to move, he took her hand again, leading her out the front door. In the distance she could hear the wail of a siren.

They climbed into the car Matt had parked at the curb and drove away, while Elizabeth looked back over her shoulder.

"She was a nice woman. She was just trying to help me, and look what happened to her."

"It shows what kind of men you're dealing with."

She nodded numbly, trying to take in his words and the

implications. She'd thought she was in trouble. She'd had no idea how much trouble. "Where are we going?"

"I don't know. But I don't think we can risk going to my apartment."

"Why?"

"They probably know I treated you. They could be looking for me, too."

She gasped. "I've gotten you into bad trouble."

"Not your fault."

"Polly's dead, and thugs with guns are after…us."

"We'll figure it out."

"How?"

"I don't know yet." He kept driving, putting distance between Polly's house and themselves.

"You sent me a message—mind to mind—and I got it."

"Yeah. Lucky thing, because I couldn't risk hitting him when he had the gun pointed at you."

"Telepathic communication," she whispered.

"Probably it only worked at that distance because it was an emergency."

She would have liked to test the theory, but not now.

Glancing at him, she asked, "You're leaving all your stuff in your apartment?"

"In Africa, I got into the habit of carrying essentials with me, in case I had to get out of a tight spot in a hurry. I've got an overnight bag in the trunk."

"Okay."

She tried to stay calm as they drove toward the suburbs.

He stopped at an ATM and got a wad of cash, then stopped at another and got more.

"What are you doing?"

"I may not be able to use my credit card after this. I want to make sure I've got money."

"Why are we running from the authorities?"

"Because we don't know the situation. The cops could be in on it."

"That's a cynical way of thinking."

"I've learned to be cynical. And I think you agree."

"Why?"

"Did you go to the cops when those guys were chasing you—or try to run away?"

"I guess I tried to run away."

He put twenty miles between Polly's house and themselves before pulling into the parking lot of a motel chain.

"Stay here. I'll be right back. And slump down in the seat so you're not so visible."

She didn't question him as she slid down and watched him disappear into the lobby. He was back in under five minutes with a key card.

"I asked for a room away from the highway," he said as he drove around to the back and pulled up in front of one of the units.

They both climbed out, and he unlocked the room. She'd held herself together in the car, but as soon as they were inside, she started to shake, leaning her shoulders against the door to stay upright.

"I'm...I'm sorry..." she managed to say through chattering teeth.

"None of this is your fault."

He reached for her, pulling her into his arms, and it was the most natural thing in the world to mold herself to his rugged frame, letting her head drop to his shoulder.

He held her close, stroking his hand up and down her back.

She knew what he was thinking. He was cussing out the bastards who had put her—the two of them—in this position. And he was determined to figure out what the hell was going on.

But she felt his coherent thoughts—and hers—slipping

away, overwhelmed by the sexual need zinging back and forth between them. It had been there from the first moment he had touched her in the hospital, a doctor thinking he was going to do a routine exam and being shocked by the results. The connection between them was stronger now, no doubt jolted up by her fear and his concern for her.

"I SHOULDN'T," HE WHISPERED. "I'm taking advantage of you."

"Do you really believe that? I mean, you can read my mind." She had to keep from punctuating the comment with a hysterical laugh.

I guess that's right."

There was more she could say, but she chose to demonstrate her feelings—and his—with actions, not words.

Twenty-four hours ago, he'd been a stranger. But that was only a technical matter. The connection between them was stronger than with anyone else she'd ever met. Since they had first touched, she'd ached to be alone with him in a bedroom. And now they were here.

The moment their mouths collided, it was like an old-fashioned kitchen match striking a rough surface. Unbearable heat flared, and she knew there was no going back—if either one of them was going to hold on to sanity. Their lips feasted on each other as his hands roamed her back.

They kissed like two lovers at the end of the world who had thought they would never see each other again. And then each of them had stumbled around a corner and found the other standing there.

Joy flooded through her. After all the long lonely years, she had found someone who...

She couldn't even put it into words. All she knew was that she and this man were on the same wavelength, both absorbed in the magical reality of being in each other's arms and each other's minds. It was so wonderful, except that the pounding in her head—which she'd felt when they had kissed in the shed—was back. "What is it?" she murmured.

"The headache?"

"Yes."

"Could be something bad."

"Or what's bad is stopping."

He made a sound of agreement, pulling her to him, deepening the kiss, angling his head to drink in everything he could.

His thoughts were there for her to read. He had wanted her for what seemed like centuries, and it was gratifying to hear that silent admission.

She moved closer, her arms creeping around his neck as she kissed him with intensity. When he finally lifted his head, they both struggled to drag in a full breath.

He reached behind her, and she knew he was turning the door lock, then slipping the safety chain into place.

They swayed as one, clinging together to keep from toppling over.

"You're putting your trust in my hands," he whispered.

"Who better?"

He must have read the invitation in her mind because he bent his head, stroking his face against her breasts, then turned to brush his lips against one of the hardened tips poking through both her thin bra and the fabric of her T-shirt.

Just that touch made heat leap inside her, and she knew that she had to get the damn shirt and bra off.

She pulled the tee over her head and reached to unhook her bra, tossing them onto the floor. By the time she'd finished, he'd pulled off his own shirt and flung it to meet hers.

Then he reached for her again, clasping her in his arms.

She cried out as her breasts pressed against his chest. The sensuality of his naked flesh against hers took her breath away.

"I don't think I can stand up much longer," she whispered.

"Likewise."

He slung his arm around her and led her to the bed, letting go of her to pull down the covers.

Then they were on the mattress, clinging, rocking in each other's arms.

He bent and swirled his tongue around one of her hardened nipples, then sucked it into his mouth.

Heat shot downward through her body, and she could only sob at the intensity of what she felt.

Yet the headache hovered at the edge of her pleasure.

"We could be heading for a cerebral hemorrhage," he muttered.

"I don't want to hear from Dr. Delano right now," she said.

And she knew he was thinking that they'd gone too far to stop.

To make that perfectly clear, she struggled out of her jeans and panties. As he caught her thoughts, he got rid of his remaining clothing. When they were both naked, he pulled her back into his arms, making her cry out again.

He slid his lips along the tender place where her ear met her cheek, dipping down to nibble along the line of her chin and then the side of her neck, before bringing his mouth back to her breast, taking one nipple into his mouth and drawing on her while his hand found its mate, using his thumb and finger to gently twist and tug, building her pleasure to fever pitch.

All her senses were tuned to him, to his masculine scent, the beat of his heart, the feel of his hair-roughened legs against her smooth ones.

Ripples of sensation flowed through her as his free hand slid down her body toward the hot, quivering core of her. Her hips moved in response, and she knew he was in her mind, sensing how good it was for her.

He rolled to his back, taking her with him, looking up at her. "You set the pace."

Maybe he still had a tiny sliver of doubt, and he was giving her the chance to back out.

She leaned in for a long, deep kiss, then raised her head so she could look down at him as she straddled his hips.

She felt the breath freeze in his chest as she lowered her body to his. She didn't need to guide him into her. They both knew where to find the right place.

For a long moment, she stared at him, overwhelmed by the intensity of her feelings. And his.

And then she began to move above him, around him, her eyes locked with his.

There was no question of hanging on to control. The pace started off fast and grew more frantic as they both pushed for climax.

The pain in her head peaked, and then it suddenly was gone, as she took them both higher and higher, and felt his hand pressed to her center to increase her pleasure.

She came undone in a burst of sensation so intense that she lost herself for a moment, but she felt him follow her over the edge, his shout of satisfaction echoing in the room.

As she collapsed against him, clinging tightly to him, he wrapped his arms around her, holding her where she was. And she was content to stay there for the next century.

Yet she couldn't. In that surge of intimacy, everything had changed.

FAR AWAY, IN LAFAYETTE, Louisiana, Rachel Harper stopped in the middle of planting flowers around the cottage where she and her husband, Jake, spent part of each week, when they weren't in New Orleans. Rachel had a boutique there, where she read tarot cards. And Jake had several businesses, including restaurants and antique shops. The cottage was on a plantation that belonged to Gabriella Boudreaux, where three couples had established a small colony. They all had something important in common. All of them were telepaths who had found each other after years of loneliness.

Recently they'd been on the run from men who wanted to use them or destroy them. Now they were living in safety and making a life for themselves. Their powers varied, but Rachel had a special ability—to send her mind over long distances. Because of that, she was always on the lookout for more couples who had hooked up. She wanted to offer them the safety she and Jake had found. Yet at the same time, she was always cautious about approaching anyone new, because the first man and woman like themselves that she and Jake had met had tried to kill them.

The last time she'd detected another couple, Jake had been with her. Now she was alone in the garden. Tension coursed through her as she looked around. When Jake didn't come rushing out, she knew he hadn't picked up on her sudden awareness that another man and woman had bonded. The other couple were far away. Somewhere on the East Coast, she thought, although she wasn't sure of the exact location. But since she was the only one here who knew about them, she could keep the information to herself and decide what to do about it later.

Chapter Seven

Elizabeth Forester, Matt said into her mind.

Thank you for that—and the rest of it.

Do you know why those men are after you?

I'm still not sure.

We'll figure it out.

He clasped her to him, holding her in place, and she was content to lie on top of him, still marveling at the way they had traveled together to an undiscovered country.

"This is what we were meant for," he murmured, absolute conviction in his voice.

She understood what he was saying.

Always incomplete.

Until now.

Why did it happen?

The loneliness or what happened when we touched?

Both.

"We have to find out," he said aloud as he stroked her arm.

She gave a short laugh. "You're saying we can't just enjoy it."

"Is that what you want to do?"

She considered the question. "No. I want to understand. And of course we still have to figure out why those men want to question me—then kill me."

"There's that."

She raised her head, looking around the room. She had barely noticed it when they'd come in. Now it had taken on meaning. It might be a typical motel room, but it was a magical place—where she and Matthew Delano had forged a connection neither one of them had ever dreamed of.

When she shifted off him, he sat up and looked around, and she knew he was following her thoughts. And she knew he was thinking about something else, as well.

Naked, he got out of bed and reached for the remote beside the television set. Then he slipped back under the covers and began flipping through the channels.

It didn't take long to find what he was looking for. The afternoon news was on several of the local channels. When he stopped at one, a reporter was standing in front of the house where they had recently escaped from Polly's killer.

"Polly Kramer, a local woman who worked as a nurse at Memorial Hospital, was found dead in her laundry room. Responding to a 9-1-1 call, police arrived to find the victim alone in the house. Wanted for questioning are Matthew Delano and a woman known only as Jane Doe, who was admitted to the hospital with amnesia. Ms. Kramer volunteered to take the discharged patient home while she tried to regain her memory. Apparently the Good Samaritan gesture led to her death."

Elizabeth stared at the television screen in shocked silence.

Matt pulled her close. "It's not your fault."

"Of course it is. She'd be alive if she hadn't volunteered to help me out."

"Don't blame yourself. You had no idea what was going to happen."

"But I knew I was in some kind of danger."

He rocked her as she shivered in his arms. "If you want to assign blame, think about how they knew where to find you. It wasn't through Polly, and it wasn't through me. It must have come from one of the other nurses."

"But why?"

"Maybe she thought she was being helpful."

Elizabeth wanted to believe she wasn't to blame, but she couldn't stop her physical reaction. "We have to find out what's going on. We have to turn him over to the police."

"But why didn't you go to the police in the first place?"

I wish I knew for sure. Maybe I didn't have enough on him. She dragged in a breath and let it out. *What if we just turned ourselves in?*

Not a good idea. If they take us into custody, we can't figure out what's going on.

Not too far away, in the home of Derek Lang, Gary Southwell and his boss were watching the same newscast.

Lang was sitting in a comfortable chair in his TV room. Southwell was standing a few feet away, shifting his weight from foot to foot and keeping his hands at his sides—away from his battered face.

"Tell me again how she got away?" Lang asked.

Gary cleared his throat, hoping his nerves didn't show. "I had a gun on her. Then she threw herself to the ground, and a guy jumped me from behind."

"Curious that she knew to get out of the line of fire."

Gary had thought about that. "He must have given her some kind of signal."

"Which would mean they had something prearranged."

Gary nodded.

"And you weren't aware of him in back of you?"

"No, sir. I had killed the old lady, and I didn't expect anyone else besides Forester."

He could see Lang thinking about the answer. He was wondering if Gary had made a mistake, or were they dealing with someone very clever? There was no use trying to persuade him either way. He'd make up his own mind.

"The police still don't know who she is, or they're not saying, which gives us an advantage," Lang mused.

"And I think she still doesn't know, either. At least I got that impression from talking to her."

"Why?"

"The look in her eyes," Gary answered promptly.

"Okay."

With any other employer, Gary might have asked a question like, "What's our next move?" but he kept silent because he knew Lang would give him further orders when he had a plan in place.

He watched his boss thinking about his options before he said, "Stake out her house. If she figures out who she is, she'll go back there."

"Yes, sir," Gary answered, relieved to have a new assignment, one he wasn't going to screw up.

"And another thing. The cops are looking for the doctor who treated her, the one on shift the morning she was released. Unless we have contradictory information, we have to assume that he's the guy who came up behind you. And we have to assume the two of them are together. Keep a man on his place, too, in case he's dumb enough to go home."

"Yes, sir."

"I'll check his credit-card records and his background. Where was he before he was in Baltimore? We may get a lead on where he's gone."

Gary left the room, feeling like he'd made a lucky escape. Other men who had worked for Derek Lang had disappeared. They might have moved on to other jobs, but Gary didn't think so.

MATT KEPT HIS ARM around Elizabeth. At the same time, he sent her soothing thoughts. It was a strange way to communicate, but he knew it was working as he felt her shivering subside.

"Let's think this through. Make some plans."

She caught a thought sliding through his head. "And you want to have a hamburger while we're doing it."

He laughed. "I can't help it. I haven't had much to eat today, and I think we both need to keep our strength up.

"Okay."

Her agreement came with what she was really thinking—that after seeing the news report, she wasn't sure she could eat.

"Inconvenient to be getting so many of your stray thoughts," he murmured.

"Yes."

"There are a ton of fast-food restaurants around here. I can go out and bring the burgers back."

"Okay," she answered, and again he picked up more than she was saying. She didn't love the idea of being left alone, but under the circumstances, it was safer. "I know," she murmured aloud.

He nodded and got dressed. "Back in a flash."

When he stopped short, she gave him a questioning look, then said, "You're worried that the cops could be looking for your car."

"Yeah."

"What are you going to do about it?"

He knew she was following all the options running through his head. He couldn't just go rent a car because he'd have to use his credit card. And stealing a car wasn't in his skill set—or his ethics set, either.

He finally said, "I read a spy novel where the hero changed a letter on his license plate with electrical tape. I'll see if I can pick some up."

When she nodded, he said, "Will you be okay?"

"Yes."

Wishing her answer were closer to the truth, he stepped outside and looked around to make sure nobody was paying him any particular attention, then drove at a moderate pace to one of the fast-food chains that were clustered in the same area as the motel complex. He bought double burgers, fries and milk shakes, because he figured both of them could use the calories.

When he returned to the room twenty minutes later, Elizabeth had dressed and had made the bed. She was watching the news again.

"Anything new?"

"No. I guess that's good."

"Yeah. Let's turn it off."

After setting the food on the table, he clicked the TV off with the remote and sat down. She took the seat opposite.

When he'd taken a few bites of his burger, he said, "I was thinking about why we're the way we are."

"So was I."

"I wonder if there's something in our backgrounds that's similar."

She laughed. "That would be easier if I *knew* my background."

"Yeah. About all we can tell is that we both felt cut off from other people." He chewed and swallowed. "Well, I'm from New Orleans. And you said you remember being there."

She nodded. "That's not much to go on. But I was thinking, the reason could be genetic. Or we could both have been exposed to some chemical—or radiation."

"Before or after we were born?"

"Did you have any major illnesses?" she asked.

"Nothing special. Only the usual."

She looked at him. "You said your mom went to a lot of trouble getting pregnant and that she went to a fertility clinic. Do you know where it was?"

"Houma, Louisiana, I think."

"That wasn't so common thirty years ago. I wonder if her

going to the clinic had something to do with it. Which leads to the question, what about me?"

"I don't know. But I can do some research in the medical databases."

"Looking for what? I don't think you're going to find telepathic abilities. Or more precisely—telepathic abilities triggered by…"

"Physical contact. With sexual relations cementing the final breakthrough."

"Very scientific."

He grinned. "I guess a medical background doesn't hurt." Sobering again, he added, "Of course, figuring out how we got telepathic powers is not our immediate problem. The way I see it, there are three things we need to do right away. Since we know your name, we can go to your house. That would help with getting your memory back. But I wouldn't suggest doing it until we have a better idea how to protect ourselves."

"With guns?"

"With our minds. When that guy was holding a weapon on you, I told you to duck, and you did it. We need to find out if we can do more stuff like that. Not just talk to each other."

"What else?"

He turned his palm up. "Did you read many science fiction stories when you were younger? There are a lot of paranormal abilities we can explore."

"I do remember *Star Trek* reruns."

"Another blast from your past."

He saw that she "heard" what that thought had triggered.

"You think we can use our minds to…blast someone?"

"I don't know. But if we can, it's a lot more convenient than having to pack a six-shooter. And stealthier, too. Who would suspect an innocent-looking woman like you of being the Terminator?"

She laughed. "Didn't the Terminator use brute force?"

"Yeah."

"Let's finish eating and try some target practice."

"Where?"

"Somewhere secluded." He waited a beat to see if she'd come up with something. Then he said, "We might drive out toward Frederick. There should be plenty of open space out there."

She took small bites of her hamburger.

"If you're not hungry, drink the milk shake."

"That's strange nutritional advice from a doctor."

He shrugged. "If we're going to try blasting something, we're probably going to use up some calories."

"I guess that's right." She took off the top of the bun and ate some of the meat and the bottom bun, then picked up the milk shake. "I can drink this while we drive."

"Do you often multitask?"

"Apparently."

"Well, eat more of your burger in the car, too."

He bundled up the trash and threw it in the wastebasket, then hesitated as he walked to the door.

"You're thinking that maybe we shouldn't come back here?"

"That could be right."

"But you're going to run out of cash if you keep renting rooms for a few hours."

"Yeah. I guess we can make a decision later."

He looked through the blinds before opening the door and ushering her to follow. They both got into the car, and he drove to the closest shopping center, which happened to have a home improvement store.

Inside, he bought electrical tape and a pair of scissors, then found a secluded part of the lot and looked at his license plate. One of the letters was an *L*, which he was able to change into an *E*. Stepping back, he looked at his handiwork. Not too bad, unless you got on top of it. But on the highway it should work. And he'd better not call attention to them by speeding.

They headed northwest on Route 70 and got off in a rural area. He found a state park where nobody else seemed to be taking advantage of nature, and they both climbed out.

"How are we going to do it?"

"Let's start with some mind-to-mind communication experiments."

"Like what?"

"When I called out to you to drop to the ground, I was about ten feet away."

"But now we've got a stronger link."

"Right," he said, and they both knew he was thinking about their lovemaking. "Let's see how far away we can do it."

"I think we have to be touching to *do it*," she teased.

"You know what I meant."

She nodded, and they first stood on opposite sides of the car.

Do you know the names of the trees? he asked.

She looked around. *I see maples, oaks, white pine.*

Good that you know them. Let's try it a little farther apart.

They each walked a few feet from the car and tried the communication again. It seemed to work until they were about twenty yards away, which was apparently the limit of their mind-to-mind communication skills.

At least for now, he said.

What do you mean?

As you pointed out, our abilities got stronger after we made love. I think that we can make everything we do stronger—if we practice.

Practice making love? she teased again, and he knew she was making an effort to lighten the situation.

That, too.

They joined up again and walked down a trail through the woods.

"It's so peaceful here. I hate the idea of destroying anything."

They came to a footbridge across a stream, where large rocks poked up through the water.

"Let's just see if we can do something to a rock," he suggested.

"How?"

He shrugged. "I don't know for sure."

She leaned on the rail, looking downstream, then pointed to a large boulder sticking above the water line. "We can aim for that one. And we don't want to work against each other. I think it might be best if one of us focuses on the rock and the other one tries to add power to the focus."

"That sounds right."

OVER A THOUSAND miles away in New Orleans, a man named Harold Goddard hunched over his computer. He was retired now, but once he'd worked for the Howell Institute, a D.C. think tank that had funded some very interesting projects over the years—like undetectable chemical weapons and torture methods that left no marks on those being interrogated.

Bill Wellington had been the director of the institute, and Harold had worked closely with him. Wellington had died in an explosion at a secret research lab in Houma, Louisiana, and that had raised Harold's interest.

The lab had been owned by Dr. Douglas Solomon, who'd run one of Wellington's pet projects, thirty some years ago. Only it hadn't quite panned out the way they'd hoped. Not one to double down on a bet, Wellington had pulled the doctor's funding, and Solomon had gone underground with a bunch of different experiments.

Had the two men kept in contact over the years? Or had Wellington found out something about the doctor's most recent activities? Harold might never find the answer to that question because Solomon and Wellington had both been killed when the doctor's hidden research facility had blown up. The authorities had concluded that the cause was a gas leak. Harold had his doubts—especially in light of subsequent events.

The lab explosion had gotten him interested in Solomon again.

He'd gone poking into old records from the clinic and had come up with a list of very interesting people—all of whose mothers had had the doctor's special treatments.

Over the past few months, Harold had brought a number of them together. Several men and women had ended up dead in bed together—apparently from cerebral vascular accidents. And then two of them, Craig Branson and Stephanie Swift, had vanished into thin air—after some very alarming incidents. Incidents that had made Harold cautious about approaching other people on the list.

Now here was one of the names—Matthew Delano, currently AWOL from his job as a house physician at Memorial Hospital in Baltimore and wanted for questioning in a murder investigation.

Harold scanned the article, noting that Dr. Delano had treated a female patient with amnesia. One of the nurses on the unit had volunteered to take Jane Doe home and had been shot to death in her own laundry room. By Delano and the woman? Or by someone else?

That was an interesting question, and one that gave Harold pause. His men had gotten caught in the cross fire when Branson had kidnapped Swift from the fortified plantation of her fiancé, John Reynard, just before the wedding ceremony.

And now here was another dangerous situation in the making, starting with the murder of the Good Samaritan nurse. Harold was tempted to send someone up to Baltimore to investigate, but perhaps it was prudent to stay away from the couple. Maybe it was best to keep tabs on the situation and make a decision later.

Yet it was hard to simply drop the chance for another experiment. He thought back over what had happened at the Reynard estate. Was there some way to protect himself from Delano and the woman—to prevent what had happened before?

Elizabeth turned to Matt. "Let me try to do the focusing."

"Because you still have a lot of memory gaps, and you want to be effective at something?"

"You read me so well."

"We already know you're effective at cooking."

"I'm not going to do in our enemies with a soufflé."

"You can make a soufflé?"

She considered the question. "Maybe not. I think I'm into more prosaic dishes—like last night's chili." The statement stopped her. "A lot has happened since last night," she murmured.

"Yes. And I also think we're stalling about trying out our powers."

"Right."

Cutting off the extraneous conversation, she looked at the rock she'd picked, thinking of a laser beam.

Or maybe lightning. And I'll try to lend a power assist.

She narrowed her eyes, concentrating—trying to do something that she had no idea how to accomplish.

Matt moved in back of her, pressing close and clasping his hands around her waist, making himself part of her.

She could feel energy flowing between them, gathering strength. It was a wonderful sensation, if she could only figure out how to use it.

Raising her hand, she stretched it toward the rock, imagining beams of power coming out of her fingers.

And suddenly, to her surprise, there was a flash of light

that streaked out toward the rock. Lightning crawled across the surface, and the water around it crackled and boiled.

She heard Matt make a strangled exclamation.

"You didn't think we could do it," she accused, "and you hid that from me."

"You think it was the wrong thing to do?" he challenged.

"No. I might not have tried if I'd known you were waffling."

"Right." He stroked his hand along her arm. "Hiding our thoughts is another skill we need to practice."

"Uh-huh." *For a whole lot of reasons,* she thought and knew he'd caught the silent comment.

She turned back to the rock, focusing on delivering another blast. This time it was easier, and the damage was more severe. She saw small chips of stone fly up into the air and land in the water. But she noticed that Matt's earlier observation was right. Blasting something took energy.

"Let's switch roles," she suggested.

He agreed, and they changed places, with her behind him clasping his waist and peeking around him to watch the rock. At the same time she tried to send him the kind of energy that he'd sent her.

She was tired, and it wasn't easy to do, but she finally felt the flow of power from her to him.

A stream of fire shot from his hand, and the rock blasted apart. She pulled him down, ducking behind the bridge rail as shards of stone flew into the air.

"Nice," she said.

"But dangerous. We need to figure out how to regulate the power," he answered.

"Can we bring it down to a little sizzle?" She pointed to another target, a tree stump that had gotten lodged in the water between two boulders. "Try to just tap it," she said. "Maybe you don't need me to do that."

Matt focused on the stump, and she felt him concentrating. After a few seconds, she saw sparks striking the surface of the bark.

"Nice," she said again. "If it were a person, I wonder how it would feel."

"Discomfort? Disorientation?"

They stayed on the bridge, leaning against the rail, both of them marveling at what they'd been doing. A few days ago, such an ability would have been unthinkable. It was empowering to realize what they could do together, but it didn't solve Elizabeth's basic problem.

"Let's go back to where we started," she said. *Memories.*

She turned so that she faced him. He wrapped her in his arms, and she leaned into him, closing her eyes as she tried to grab on to something from her past.

She knew Matt was keeping the exchange directed away from himself, trying to help her dig out nuggets from her past.

The easiest memories to reach were from her childhood. And not all of them were bad. She remembered being enchanted by a trip to the zoo with her parents. She remembered a trip to Disney World where she'd insisted on riding the Space Mountain roller coaster. She remembered being the best girl basketball player in her high school class. And then she remembered the time she had missed a shot and lost a playoff game for the team.

Matt rubbed her arm. "Don't focus on that."

"I felt horrible. I had finally found something that made me valuable to the other kids, and I blew it."

"We all have stuff like that."

The next picture that came to her knocked the breath from her lungs. It was like when Matt had hypnotized her. She saw young women huddled together. Only now she felt their fear and knew that she was the only one who could save them from a horrible fate.

Chapter Eight

Who are they? Matt asked.

"I don't know," she almost shouted in her frustration as the mental image faded. "But they're depending on me, and I have to help them."

"Okay," he answered, giving her his full support. "But how do we do it?"

"First I have to figure out who they are—and where they are." She swallowed hard. "And I think there might be something at my house that tells me."

He gave her a long look. "You think it's safe to go to your house? You might not know why those men were chasing you, but it's a given that they know your name. Now that you've escaped from them twice, they probably have your house staked out—hoping you'll come back."

"I know that." She dragged in a frustrated breath and let it out. "But I think I have to. I mean, I can't just keep running away. I have to figure out what's going on."

"Inconvenient," he answered in a dry voice that might have fooled her if she hadn't already learned a lot about him.

"I probably have records on my computer."

"And somebody probably already got to them—after the car accident, when you were out of commission."

She nodded, hating that they were in this bind. She needed to know more about herself, and she knew she couldn't do it alone. She also knew that Matt was following her thought processes.

"We have your address, and we can get there."

"We'll go back there, but we have to be cautious," he said.

It was instructive to see the way he thought as they drove toward Arbutus, a middle-class community, where her house was located. He stopped at a drugstore and bought them both Orioles baseball caps, which they pulled down low to hide their faces. He also bought two Orioles T-shirts. Hers was oversize, and hung far down her arms and body, but it certainly created a different look for her. A roll of duct tape completed his purchases.

When they'd returned to his car and she'd put the shirt over her clothing, he said, "Lie down in the back."

She didn't have to ask why. She knew he wanted anyone watching to think that a lone man was driving through the neighborhood.

Prone on the backseat, she couldn't see any details of the passing scenery, but that didn't matter because she didn't remember the details, anyway.

"I just drove past your house," he informed her.

"What's it look like?"

"It's a two-story. An older home with a porch and new vinyl siding. The front yard is nicely planted, and there's a man sitting in a car across the street, keeping an eye on the place."

"Great."

"It's the thug who killed Polly."

She sucked in a sharp breath. "Oh, Lord."

"We expected him or someone like him."

"Too bad we can't tell the cops he's here."

"Yeah. But it would just be his word against ours. And I have the feeling he'd lawyer up and get out before we could blink."

She nodded, then said, "He was alone when he came to Polly's, but he's not going to make that mistake again. I'm sure there's another guy out back."

"And we can't drive up the alley, because we could get trapped."

"Right."

He turned the corner and parked near the end of the alley. They both got out, walking back. She didn't even know which house she lived in, and it was strange to have Matt be the one to direct her.

He pointed. "Your place is about halfway down."

The yards were about thirty feet deep, all of them with three-foot-high chain-link fences.

She spotted the other man when they were about twenty yards away. He was sitting on her back steps, partly screened by low bushes.

We have to get close enough and disable him before he can alert his friend out front.

I don't suppose you remember who lives in the house next door.

Sorry. But in this neighborhood, they're probably at work. Let's hope.

Before they turned in at the house to the right of hers, they planned their attack. As they walked toward the back door, Elizabeth could see the guy on her back steps flick them a look, but apparently he didn't recognize either one of them.

When they reached the door, Matt pretended to get out his keys. She pressed close to him, giving him energy as he raised his arm toward the intruder on her back steps.

Is this going to work? I mean, he's not a rock in a stream. We'll find out.

She felt Matt gathering power, then sending a bolt of energy toward the man on her back steps. It made the guy go rigid, then slump to the side. Matt was already charging down the steps and vaulting the fence into her yard.

Instead of continuing with the superhero route, he socked the guy in the jaw, then took the gun from his shoulder holster, checked that the safety was on, and stuffed the weapon into the waistband of his jeans, under his Orioles T-shirt.

She helped pull the thug into the bushes, where they taped his hands and feet together and slapped a piece of tape over his mouth. They also took his cell phone and wallet.

Matt took the battery out of the phone, then pawed through the wallet. The guy had a wad of cash, but no identification.

"The money will come in handy," Matt said, as he stuffed the bills into his own pocket. "Do you keep a key to the back door somewhere?"

"I wish I knew. Maybe a neighbor has a key, but I don't recall."

She pushed aside a flowerpot and moved a couple of large rocks but saw nothing.

"We may have to break in." Matt climbed the steps and tried her door. When it turned out to be unlocked, she drew in a sharp breath.

"Obviously the bad guys have been inside and didn't bother to lock up. Stay here until I make sure nobody's inside."

He drew the gun and held it in both hands. Before stepping inside, he studied the threshold, looking for trip wires, then cautiously entered.

Matt had asked her to wait for his all clear, but as she stood with her heart pounding in her chest, she knew she couldn't make herself stay outside. This was her house—an important key to understanding herself. And really, would the bad guys have someone in here, when they already had a man at the front and back?

When Matt saw she was following him, he made a rough sound, but he didn't order her out.

"Wait downstairs while I go up."

"Okay."

Again, waiting was hard.

All clear, he told her as he came down the stairs.

But I see from your thoughts that it's a mess up there. Sorry.

She had expected it from what she saw on the first floor. As she looked around, she grappled with mixed reactions. She was anxious to see the place where she lived. Apparently her taste ran to the whimsical, with touches like bright cloths on horizontal surfaces and ethnic pottery—not much like that sober black jacket and slacks she'd been wearing when she had had the accident. It seemed she liked to kick back when she got into her own environment.

But at the same time she was thinking about her taste, she was taking in the destruction. Someone had been through the house, searching and not caring what kind of mess they left.

She hurried to her office, which was a long, narrow room at the side of the house, and gasped when she saw her computer. The screen lay smashed on the floor and the processor had been taken apart, presumably to remove the hard drive.

The room was divided into two sections by a bank of filing cabinets. Behind them was an area she'd blocked off as a storage closet where she'd piled cardboard boxes purchased from an office supply store. From the mess on the floor she gathered that some had held old tax information and financial records, while others were for books and storage of out-of-season clothing. After looking at the area behind the cabinets, she walked through the main part of the office, where files and papers lay all over the floor.

As she looked toward the stairs, she was suddenly able to picture her cozy bedroom. She'd painted it blue and white, and continued the theme with the curtains and bedspread. She knew it was better not to go up and look at the mess, and better not to go up there and get trapped.

With a grimace, she returned to the kitchen, picked up a set of measuring spoons from the floor and looked around. Oak cabinets. Ceramic tile on the floor and some kind of fake stone on the countertops. The room looked like it had been renovated in the past five years, but it was as wrecked as the office. Cabinet doors hung open, and food had been emptied out, as though someone had thought she might hide important information in a cereal box.

Matt joined her.

"Sorry. It looks like they would have found anything of value."

"Maybe not," she muttered.

The searchers had taken apart all the obvious places, but was she clever enough to have thought of somewhere they wouldn't have considered?

Like, would she have hidden something in a box of tampons? Probably not, because every spy knew that old trick.

After returning to the office, she looked around and saw a bulletin board. Excitement leaped inside her when she saw several name tags from conferences hanging on pins.

"I'm a social worker," she breathed.

"Looks like it."

She swallowed hard. "I guess we have that in common—taking jobs where we could help people, because that was the only way we could connect."

"Yeah."

She picked up a framed diploma from the floor. "And I have a master's degree from the University of Maryland."

"Which might mean you grew up in the area—or not. It could be that they had the kind of program you were looking for."

Matt walked into the closet area. When she heard him open the window, she poked her head around the filing cabinets.

"What are you doing?"

"What I learned to do in Africa. Making sure there's an alternative exit if we need it."

GARY SOUTHWELL LOOKED at his watch. He and Hank Patterson had been staking out Elizabeth Forester's house since he'd gotten his new orders from Mr. Lang. They were supposed to check in with each other every half hour, and Patterson hadn't phoned. Which was unsettling because the man had been punctual as clockwork until this time.

Southwell clicked the phone one more time, trying to get his partner. Finally he gave up and wondered what he should do. Not call Lang. His boss was already annoyed by their lack of progress in apprehending Elizabeth Forester. The woman had determination—and grit. He'd give her that. And apparently she'd found a guy who wasn't going to leave her twisting in the wind.

Had they known each other before she landed in the hospital or what? If not, it was shocking that the doctor was laying his life on the line for a woman he'd met only a few days ago. Gary sure wouldn't do it. He laughed. Or for any other broad. They simply weren't worth it.

He slipped out of the car where he'd been sitting for hours and looked around as he stretched, then started down the block, glancing back at the house before turning the corner. If Forester and the doctor were in there, he was giving them the chance to get out the front, but on balance, he had to risk it.

In the alley, he hurried to the back door, where Patterson was supposed to be stationed. He wasn't there, but as Gary approached the house, he heard a muffled sound of distress in the bushes. When he cautiously approached, he found his partner lying on the ground, taped hand and foot.

Gary pulled the tape off his mouth. "What the hell happened to you?"

"They got the drop on me."

"You mean Elizabeth and that doctor?"

"Yeah," Patterson said as Gary freed his partner's wrists and started working on his legs.

Patterson shook his hands and kicked his feet to get the circulation going.

"What happened, exactly?"

"I'm not sure. It was like…" He stopped and glanced at Gary. "Like they hurled a thunderbolt or something at me."

"That's impossible. Maybe they had a Taser gun."

Patterson considered the idea. "I don't know what it was. I'm just sayin', be damned careful if you get near them."

"Were you unconscious?"

"Maybe for a little while."

"Okay," Gary muttered, wondering what they were going to do now and thinking about that five-minute window when he'd left his post and headed back here—to find Patterson.

Could they have gotten away while his partner was out?

"Did you see them leave?" Gary asked.

"I don't think so."

"Then we'd better assume they saw me out front, which means they wouldn't go out that way." Gary glanced at Patterson. "You steady on your feet?"

"Steady enough to kill those bastards."

"Waste the guy. The boss wants to do the woman himself."

"You mean do her—then kill her?"

"Yeah."

IN THE OFFICE, Elizabeth picked up some of the papers scattered on the floor and thumbed through them. "These are records of some of my clients."

After righting the desk chair, she sat down and started to read one of the cases. "This woman was living in a flophouse in Baltimore. It looks like she came into the country illegally."

"I know you want to understand what you were doing, but I think you don't have time to read cases now."

She gave him an exasperated look. "They could be clues

to what was going on—when those thugs tried to grab me after the accident."

"Maybe you can take some with you. We've got to get out of here pretty fast."

She nodded but didn't move.

"There's got to be something here," she murmured as she looked around the shambles that had been her office. "Something they missed."

"How do you know?"

She shrugged. "I just do. And maybe you can help me figure it out."

Standing, she reached for Matt. Pulling him close, she molded her body against his as they stood in the middle of the mess. His arms stroked up and down her back, and as she held on to him, she felt the familiar merging of their minds that had so quickly become necessary to her existence.

Yes, he silently agreed.

She wanted to simply revel in the special closeness they shared, but she knew there wasn't time for that now. What she had to do was search for the memories he'd brought back to her. Not something long ago. Something recent.

Eyes closed, she mentally looked around the room trying to figure out what she couldn't remember on her own.

Her mental gaze shifted to the bulletin board. There were several whimsical things stuck to it including a couple greeting cards, a Mardi Gras mask, two cocktail swizzle sticks and a key ring with a small flashlight attached.

Matt followed her thoughts as she stepped away from him and reached for the key ring. She had just taken it down from the board when an unwelcome noise made them both go still.

In the quiet of the house, they heard the front door open.

Chapter Nine

Matt froze. He'd known all along that coming to Elizabeth's place was taking a chance, but he'd also been desperate to help her get more information about herself. Now it appeared that they'd run out of luck. He looked at Elizabeth, seeing the terror on her face—and also the anger. These guys kept coming after her like a relentless robot killer in a science-fiction movie, and now one or more of them were in the house with them.

Stealthy footsteps crept slowly down the hall.

What are we going to do? Elizabeth asked.

Get out the escape hatch.

Thank God you thought of one.

He ushered Elizabeth behind him. *Climb out the window.*

What about you?

I'll block them, then follow. Head for the car.

He knew she wanted to argue about the hastily conceived plan, but she silently acknowledged there was no alternative.

Stepping around the filing cabinets, she headed for the open window.

He pulled out the gun that he'd taken away from the guy they'd encountered out back. What had happened while they were inside, exactly? Had Polly's killer found his partner and set him free? Or had the guy out front come around back? And did whoever was out there know Matt was armed?

Matt tensed as the footsteps came closer, his attention divided between Elizabeth and the invaders. In his mind he could see her climbing out the window and dropping down to the narrow space between her house and the one next door.

When he knew she was outside, he breathed out a small sigh. She was safely out of the house, but he knew the man who had killed Polly Kramer wouldn't hesitate to do the same to Matthew Delano.

"We know you're in there," one of the thugs called out. "Come out with your hands up, and you won't be hurt."

Oh, sure.

Could they really know he was in here? Or were they guessing? Apparently they didn't remember there was a back way out of the room. But Matt couldn't just run for it. If they came through the door, they could catch him on the way out and drill him in the back.

To give himself a few extra seconds, Matt fired through the doorway.

Curses rang behind him—the voices telling him there were at least two guys out there—as he ducked into the area behind the filing cabinets.

One of the men in the hall fired an answering shot through the door.

Matt reached the window and was thankful that Elizabeth had pushed it open farther. Climbing halfway out, he returned fire before hurling himself through the opening.

He wasn't surprised to find Elizabeth waiting for him on the ground. Even without reading her thoughts, he knew she wasn't going to take off and leave him there.

Thank God. Her exclamation of relief rang in his head as he pressed his shoulder to hers.

He didn't waste his breath or his mental energy upbraiding her for staying in the path of danger. Instead, he focused on the window, knowing she was following his thoughts and lending him power. When a head appeared above them, Matt hurled a bolt of energy at the man, who made a wheezing sound and dropped back inside.

Come on.

With Elizabeth right behind him, Matt ran down the narrow side passage, then climbed over the waist-high fence between the two houses, reaching to help her over.

They sprinted through the yard, through the back gate and down the alley.

No shots followed, presumably because the guys weren't going to take a chance on a gun battle outdoors in a residential neighborhood. Or maybe they were worried about Matt's secret weapon.

But he and Elizabeth weren't exactly home free. Before they'd reached the end of the alley, a police siren sounded in the distance.

"Someone must have heard the shooting in your house," he said as he slowed his pace, walking at normal speed toward his car.

Moments later, they were inside the vehicle and on their way out of the neighborhood, leaving the cops and the thugs behind them.

Elizabeth sat rigidly in her seat, and Matt knew what was in her mind. He was torn between escaping and giving her the reassurance they both needed.

He turned onto a side street, made another turn, and pulled up under a low-hanging maple tree that partially hid them from the street.

When he cut the engine, she turned to him with a little sob that was part relief and part frustration. He slid his seat back and reached for her, pulling her into his arms, holding tight as he ran his hands over her back and shoulders, thankful that they had both made it out of her house alive.

Her apology rang in his mind.

I'm so sorry.

Not your fault.

You said it was too dangerous to go there.

But I also said we had to do it. We both knew it was necessary.

They almost caught us.

But they didn't.

As they silently spoke, she brought her mouth to his for a frantic kiss. And his response was no less emotional. If they hadn't been on a public street, he knew they would have been tearing each other's clothing off in the next moment and making frenzied love.

But here in the car in a residential neighborhood, all they could do was clutch tightly, kissing and touching and silently proclaiming how glad they were that they'd found each other and how relieved they were that they'd escaped from Derek Lang's men.

The name jolted through both of them. He knew that the heightened emotions of the moment had made it pop into Elizabeth's head. But he also knew from her thoughts that she was sure it was right. He was the man who'd sent the thugs after her—when she'd crashed her car, then later at Polly Kramer's house and now. She looked at Matt, and he caught the swell of victory pounding through her.

Derek Lang. That's his name, she shouted in his mind.

Yes.

The next question is, what did I do to him?

I hope we've got the answer.

She nodded as she reached into her pocket and pulled out the small flashlight that she'd taken from the bulletin board. The men who'd searched the house had ignored it as just part of her kitschy office decorations, but when she'd unscrewed the top, she pulled out the thumb drive hidden inside.

"They got the hard drive, but they didn't get this," she said. "Hopefully it duplicates what was in the computer."

"Clever of you."

She grinned at him. "Yes, if I do say so myself."

"Let's hope it's got what we need. I'd like to figure out what's going on."

"But we need a computer." She smiled as she caught his next thought and murmured, "Your laptop is in your trunk."

"Yeah."

"Clever of *you* to bring it along."

"I thought it might come in handy."

She didn't ask where they were going because he knew she saw the picture of the motel room that had formed in his mind.

She scooted back to the other side of the car. He slid his seat closer to the wheel again and drove away, being careful to stay under the speed limit.

Matt slowed at the row of fast-food restaurants where they'd bought lunch.

"We just used up a lot of energy with that mental stuff. We should get something to eat," he said.

She tipped her head toward him. "That might be what came out of your mouth, but you were thinking about something else."

"I guess I can't hide that X-rated image of the two of us in bed. But we've got to keep our priorities straight. Food, work and then pleasure. What do you want for dinner?"

When a picture of a large pizza, loaded with cheese, vegetables and meat, leaped into her mind, he said, "Excellent choice."

They bought the pizza along with soft drinks and brought it back to the motel.

MATT DROVE THROUGH the lot before he stopped, but as far as he could tell, nobody suspicious was hanging around. Still he had Elizabeth wait in the car while he retrieved the laptop from the trunk.

After he'd ushered her inside, he set the computer and

the food on the table, then locked the door and checked out the bathroom.

"There's a window in here," he announced.

"In case we have to make another quick getaway?"

"I'm just being cautious."

"It was lucky you were being cautious at my house."

They looked at each other for a long moment. *We have to practice restraint and discipline,* he forced himself to say.

Opening the box, he selected a slice of pizza and put it on a paper plate while he booted up his computer.

He looked over and saw Elizabeth watching him.

"You can just eat like that—after someone's tried to kill you?"

"That's the best time for a hearty meal."

She shook her head and reached for a slice, pulling her chair around to his side of the table so she could look at the screen while she ate.

"Okay, this is good," she admitted.

He inserted the thumb drive into the USB port. They both ate pizza and sipped their drinks while they waited for the start-up routine to complete.

"What do you think is on the drive?" he asked.

"I don't know. Too bad it's not my biography."

"Since we know your name, I'm sure we can get an approximation. There's probably a bio of you at the place where you work. Maybe one of the county or city social service agencies."

"I didn't think of that. But let's read the thumb drive first."

He switched the computer's attention to the external drive and got a list of files.

"Which one's first?"

"Might as well start at the top."

The first file contained snapshots of women—all of whom looked like they might be of Eastern European origin.

Next was a picture of the Port of Baltimore and one of

the huge containers that was often taken off ships and set directly onto tractor-trailer trucks.

They both stared at the pictures.

"It might seem far-fetched, but I think I understand the connection between the pictures," Elizabeth said. "Does it sound crazy to think that Derek Lang is using cargo containers to smuggle women illegally into the country?" She swallowed hard. "And then something bad happens to them?"

"Well, we know something big is going on. Big enough for Derek Lang to want you out of the picture."

"As in—dead."

"You must have found out about it. But how could you stumble onto something like that?"

She shook her head in frustration.

They opened more files. Some contained dates and times. Others were lists that looked like order forms.

They kept looking through the files, but there was no more information that helped Elizabeth unravel the mystery.

"We have to help these women," she murmured. "Which means we have to figure out where they are."

"And we have to help ourselves, because we're not going to be safe unless Derek Lang is off our backs." He turned toward her. "I wonder why you didn't just go to the police."

"There has to be a reason."

When Elizabeth looked at Matt, she knew he had caught her thoughts about how to come up with more information about the women.

The first time I remembered anything about myself was when you touched me. I think we need to try that again.

He nodded, but she was pretty sure it was going to take more than simply holding hands.

Keeping her eyes on him, she stood up and kicked off her shoes and watched him do the same.

"You think we're going to be able to focus on what we're supposed to be doing?" she asked.

"I guess we'll find out. Keep your shorts on to make it harder to go too far."

"A good precaution."

She pulled off her shirt, bra and jeans, leaving on her panties, and when she pulled back the covers and slipped into bed, he followed her, wearing only his briefs. He drew her to him, both of them longing for the contact and both of them knowing that they couldn't give in to their own needs—not yet. They had to focus on dragging out the information that had to be in her mind.

She brushed her lips against his, then pillowed her head on his shoulder, while his hands stroked over her arms, and up and down her back.

Maximum contact, he silently murmured as he lifted her up and stretched her out on top of himself, only two layers of fabric separating her center from his erection.

The intimacy was like a jolt of heat, and she couldn't stop herself from moving against him. After a few moments, he quieted her with his hands and thoughts.

Stay still, or we'll end up making love instead of pulling information from your mind.

Hard to remember that's what we're supposed to be doing. Yeah.

Knowing he was right, she settled down, letting the simmering sexual heat pull their minds deeply together. The first time they'd touched, the transfer of memories had been unexpected. Now they had a much better idea of what they were doing—like when she'd found the thumb drive hanging in plain sight on the bulletin board.

And now he wasn't just inviting her memories. She felt him lending her energy, the way he'd done when they were out in the woods hurling thunderbolts at rocks, and then again when they had disabled the guy who had staked out the back of her house.

As she pulled the power into herself, another picture formed in her mind.

She was at a row house in Baltimore, checking out how things were going with a young mother named Wendy, who'd adopted a child from Romania. They had been talking for about five minutes when another young woman slipped in the back door.

Elizabeth looked up, taking in the woman's frightened eyes and pale skin. The newcomer and the mom exchanged glances.

"This is Sabrina. I met her when I was out walking the baby. I saw her a few times, and I knew she needed help. I told her you'd be here today—and that you could help her."

Elizabeth nodded, wondering at this unorthodox approach to social services. But in her profession, she had to be open to people in need, even when they didn't necessarily go through normal channels.

Wendy picked up her baby and went upstairs, leaving Elizabeth alone with the other woman.

"How can I help you?" she asked.

Sabrina licked her lips and spoke haltingly in heavily accented English. "Pardon me if I don't speak too good."

"You're doing fine."

"I thought to come to this country because there is nothing for me back home." She stopped and swallowed hard. "I had some money saved. I paid it to a man who said he could get me into America—and get me a good job."

When she stopped talking, Elizabeth prompted her. "And what happened?"

"He got me here. Me and other women. We traveled in a big shipping container."

"My Lord."

"It wasn't so bad. We had light in there, and food and

toilets. But then we got to Baltimore, and I found it was all a big lie. Men were here to meet us. They took us to a house where they forced us…" She stopped then started again. "Forced us to be prostitutes."

Elizabeth sucked in a sharp breath. "I'm sorry."

"They had us under guard, at a house way out in the country, but I was able to escape."

"How?"

"A man wanted to take me home for the weekend. He paid a lot of money for that, and I hit him over the head, stole some of his money and got away. I know that attacking him and stealing from him was wrong, but I had to do it."

"What he was doing was wrong."

Sabrina nodded. "Yes."

"But why is this happening in Baltimore?"

"Some of the girls had relatives in the city. That's why they came here. We had talked about this area, and I knew the part of the city where people from my country lived. I found this neighborhood. I was starving on the street, and Wendy helped me." She gave Elizabeth a pleading look. "I need to hide out from the man who is in charge of this shameful business. And I need to get the other girls out of that house."

Elizabeth was shuddering as she came back to the present. Tears leaked from her eyes as she looked down at Matt.

He rolled to his side, cradling her against himself. "You were investigating the smuggling ring."

"Yes."

"And it led you to Derek Lang."

"Yes. Sabrina had picked up his name at the bordello."

"Why didn't you turn him over to the cops?"

"Because I went to a fancy reception where he was. I saw him with a man who's high up in the police department, and I knew he was paying the guy off to look the other way. I was afraid that if I just turned him in, I'd end up dead."

"Which looks like it was the plan anyway."

"Obviously Lang found out I was poking into his business. I was staying in a motel room near home, while I figured out what to do." She made a low sound. "I left some of my stuff there."

"Like what?"

"Clothing. Toilet articles." She thought for a moment. "I guess nothing that would help them find me now."

"Right."

"When you didn't come back, the management probably went in and cleared it out."

"Did they save it, do you think?"

"Is there something important in your stuff?"

She laughed. "I did have some money."

"We'll have to think about whether it's worth trying to retrieve it—and paying your back rent."

"If we explain that I lost my memory, maybe they'll be… charitable."

"Maybe, but we've got more important issues."

"Yes. Like my car crash." She shook her head. "It's not my car. Susan, one of my coworkers, lent it to me because she was going out of the country and wouldn't need it."

"When this is over, we'll figure out what to do about that."

"I suddenly remember a lot more stuff."

"Good."

She gave him a direct look. "Well, it's not exactly coming at a convenient time. I mean I want to explore what I know about myself, but we can't while we're stuck in this mess."

"You remember something specific that you think is important?"

"Yes. You said your mother went to a fertility clinic in Houma, Louisiana."

"Yes."

"Would you believe, I remember *my* mother talking about it?"

"You do?"

She nodded. "That's the link we've been looking for between us. It can't be a coincidence. It has to have something to do with our abilities."

"But first we have to deal with Lang and his thugs."

"Yes. I know they would have gotten me when I crashed the car, but I think there were too many people around." She dragged in a breath and let it out. "And now what are we going to do—about us and the women?"

DEREK LANG RARELY permitted himself to be worried. He was a visionary, but he was also a cautious man, with a firm handle on any situation into which he ventured. But this thing with Elizabeth Forester was getting out of hand.

Lang had investigated Dr. Delano and found out he'd done several years as a medic in Africa—during which he'd had a number of hair-raising escapes from death. Apparently those experiences had taught him how to defend himself.

He looked at Patterson, the man who'd been tasked with guarding Forester's back door.

"How did they get past you?" he asked.

"They zapped me with something."

"Zapped?"

"Something like a Taser."

Derek's brow wrinkled. A Taser wasn't exactly a long-distance weapon.

He asked for an account of the rest of the screwed-up mission, listening as Southwell related finding Patterson and then they both went into the house after the fugitives, one from the front and one from the back.

"And how did they get out of that?"

"The doctor opened a window while they were in the office."

Lang thought of saying that every exit should have been covered, but of course, there had only been two guys on the scene. Even so, he wanted to lash out at these men who had come back to him with bad news, but he wasn't going to waste the energy. And he'd better start looking for a replacement for Southwell. The man was simply making too many mistakes.

"Double the guard on The Mansion," he said.

"Yes, sir."

"And tell Susanna to come in here," he ordered.

She would do what she could to calm his frayed nerves.

Chapter Ten

"I'm thinking," Matt answered.

He didn't have to say more, because he knew Elizabeth was tapping in to his mental processes.

She went very still, when she realized what he had in mind. "Find the house?" she asked.

"Yeah."

She pressed her hand to her mouth, her face a study in concentration. "I...don't know where it is." Panic bloomed on her features. "Oh, Lord, Matt. What if all this has been for nothing?"

He wasn't going to simply give up. When he held out his arms, she hesitated for a moment, then came into them. He could feel her panic subsiding as she leaned into him. *Is the house in the city?*

I don't think so.

But you saw it?

Yes. I'm pretty sure I snuck up on it.

Let's go back there.

They both closed their eyes, and he pressed his cheek to hers, flooding power into her the way he had learned to do. For long moments he felt her frustration, until a picture of a large dwelling formed in her mind.

It was a Victorian mansion with three floors, a wide front porch and a newer wing on either side. It was painted a tasteful beige with darker trim. At one side he saw a paved lot where several high-end cars were parked. A brick path led from the lot to the front door. And the grounds around the house were nicely landscaped with azaleas, dogwoods and other typical local greenery.

That's it?

Yes. You'd never dream it was anything but a pretty rural residence. She gave a harsh laugh. *Or maybe an upscale bed-and-breakfast.*

How did you get close?

I waited until it was getting dark, then parked down the road and came through the woods.

You didn't get inside?

No. But I looked in the windows.

She stayed with the scene, and he got more than visual effects. From inside the house he heard soft jazz drifting toward him. It was accompanied by another picture that came to him of young pretty women wearing dressing gowns. Some were standing, others sitting in a nicely furnished room where men in sport shirts and slacks relaxed with drinks.

One of the men stood and held out his hand to a blond woman. She swallowed hard, then got up and walked ahead of him out of the room. He saw the man caress her bottom through her gown, saw her wince, then caught a glimpse of the couple climbing the stairs before they disappeared from sight.

He picked up the disgust in Elizabeth's memory as she backed away from the house and hurried across the neatly trimmed lawn. Turning around, she looked at the building again and froze. For the first time, she spotted a security camera she hadn't seen earlier. With a little gasp, she ran for the woods at the side of the house. But knew it was already too late.

"They must have seen you," he said aloud.

"Yes. I wasn't thinking about cameras. I only wanted to make sure that Sabrina was telling the truth." She made a soft moaning sound. "Oh, Lord, and I thought I was being so careful."

"Go back to the scene," he said.

He felt her resistance. She didn't want to go anywhere near the upscale prison where young women were being forced to service men who were willing to pay for the pleasure, but she did it because they were trying to save the women. Her head lay on his shoulder, but her mind flashed back to the memory, and he saw from her point of view as she ran frantically into the darkened woods. It took a few moments for her eyes to adjust to the gloom, and she stepped into a patch of brambles that tore at her clothing.

She wrenched herself away and veered to the left as she kept running, madly fleeing the house. And now he heard the sounds of heavy footsteps crashing through the underbrush after her.

"There she is."

"Don't let her get away."

Fear leaped inside her and kept her running as fast as she could. When a tree root snagged her foot, she almost crashed to the ground but caught herself against a tree and kept moving. She was breathing hard when she reached her car, opened the door with the remote and threw herself inside.

She gunned the engine and sped out of the woods, skidding as she turned right, then hurtled down the road, but Matt and she both knew she hadn't been in the clear.

When he felt her trembling, he soothed her. "It's okay."

"I made a mess of that."

"No. You got a look at the bordello—at what was going on in there."

Silently he asked her to return to the vision once again. She shook her head, hating to revisit the scene.

I think we can get information we need.

How?

Try it again. Get back into the car—when you were speeding away just now.

She put herself back into the vehicle. When she was sure she'd lost the pursuers, she slowed. Coming to a street sign, she saw she was on Sparks Road, and the cross street was York Road.

He squeezed her shoulder. "I think you've got it."

"Yes."

When she caught what was in his mind, she went rigid. "No."

"Yes. We have to make sure it's still business as usual out there."

"Then what?"

"I think I know what will work, but we have to make sure about the place."

He held her for a few moments longer, pulling her closer.

They'd both wanted to make love, yet now that she remembered the fate of the women Lang had forced into sexual slavery, neither one of them was in the mood for lovemaking.

And again they didn't have to discuss anything out loud. They each knew what the other was thinking.

Finally he slipped away from her and sat up. "Come on." He felt her terror and also her determination. "You won't be alone."

"After everything that's happened, it's the only reason I can do it, I think."

Matt went to his computer and looked up the roads he'd seen in her mind.

They were in Harford County, and he mapped a route to the York and Sparks Roads.

He knew she didn't want to go back there, but he also understood she had steeled herself to do what was necessary to bring down Derek Lang.

They drove north, and he followed her previous route in reverse. The farther they got up York Road, the more he could feel her tension. But she said nothing as he drove past the entrance to the house, which was on a two-lane rural road off Overbrook.

They came to a long drive with a small sign that said The Mansion. The house itself was up a long driveway, and you could barely see the house through the trees.

"Nice and private for the men who like to get their jollies here," he said.

"And hard for the girls to escape. They probably don't even know how close they are to the city." She shuddered. "I can't imagine how it is for them. They pay money to get out of their countries, and they're full of hope, thinking they're coming to something better. Then they end up *here*."

"You're going to get them out of the mess they're in."

"But Lang didn't just start with this shipment. He's been bringing in women for years. How many others did he lure here? And what happened to them?"

Knowing she was having trouble coping with the pain of the revelations, Matt reached over and covered her hand. "We can only deal with the situation that exists now."

"I know."

Getting back to practicalities, he said, "Last time, you parked on the other side of the property."

"Yes."

"Then let's go in from this side."

"Do you think they'll be looking for us?"

"Hard to say. Since you returned to your house, you could have your memory back. But they smashed your computer, so they may assume you can't find this location again."

"Let's hope that's what they think."

He pulled onto a dirt track and under some low-hanging trees that hid the car, then turned to Elizabeth.

"We need to make sure it's business as usual there. And we need to make sure nobody sees us, because if they do, they may well move the women."

"Yes."

It was getting dark, as it had been the first time Elizabeth had come here. This time they walked cautiously through the woods, being careful to make as little noise as possible.

Matt looked back the way they'd come, thinking that they might be in a hurry on the return trip.

When they got to the edge of the trees, he squeezed Elizabeth's hand.

"How far is the range of the cameras?" she asked.

"Probably not far, since they want to concentrate on the grounds near the house."

They were about fifty yards away, and they both stayed in the shadows under the trees as they looked toward the well-maintained structure.

"Quite a setup," Matt murmured.

"Nothing but the best for Lang's guests. Do you think he's actually here?" she asked.

"Probably not. He may steer clear of this place. I'm going to have a look. You stay here."

"Okay."

He caught the ambivalence in her mind. She hated sending him closer, yet she didn't want to get near the house herself.

Lamps were on all over the first floor. As in Elizabeth's earlier memory, light jazz drifted toward them. As he moved toward the house, he looked up and saw the nearest camera. Focusing on it, he sent a burst of energy toward it. When he heard a zapping sound, he knew he'd taken care of that problem.

Still he waited for any sign that he'd been spotted. Like on Elizabeth's previous trip, he had a good view in through the windows. He saw casually dressed men looking like they were at a party, a well-dressed older woman who must be the hostess, and women in nightwear who looked out of place in the expensively furnished rooms.

Having confirmed that this was the right location, he

was about to turn around and head back to the woods when he heard Elizabeth crying out a warning inside his mind.

Watch out.

But it was already too late. In the next moment, a rough voice ordered, "Hold it right there and raise your hands above your head."

With a silent curse, Matt stopped in his tracks, upbraiding himself for being too focused on the view inside the building.

"Turn around," the rough voice ordered.

There was no real choice, since running for it would only get him a bullet in the back. He turned and found himself facing a bald man dressed in a dark shirt and slacks. It wasn't anyone he recognized from his previous brushes with Lang's thugs.

"We're going inside," Baldy said.

Matt eyed him, thinking that he could send a bolt of power at the guy, but that was dangerous with the man's finger on the trigger of a gun pointed at Matt.

And then he heard Elizabeth's voice in his head, telling him what he'd told her back at Polly Kramer's house.

Drop to the ground.

She was fifteen yards away, and he didn't know if she could reach the guy from there. But he did what she said, watching the man with the gun gasp and topple over. And luckily, he didn't alert anyone else by pulling the trigger as he went down.

Elizabeth sprinted out of the woods. Matt clicked the safety on the gun and set it on the man's abdomen. Together they dragged the guy across the lawn and under the trees.

Matt turned to look back the way they'd come. As far as he could see, no one else had noticed the capture.

Thanks, he said to Elizabeth.

I should have seen him sooner, but I was focused on you. She looked down at the guy, who was about Matt's height, with bulging muscles and a swarthy complexion. *What are we going to do? You said that if anyone saw us, they might shut down the operation out here.*

Yeah. I'm thinking.

Can we...zap his brain or something?

It might do him permanent damage.

Do you care?

He considered the question. He was a doctor, dedicated to treating illness and injury. But in Africa he'd gotten used to the truth that if someone was trying to do you harm, you might have to beat him to the punch.

No, he answered.

How do we do it?

Aim a blast at his head, he said, then considered the answer more carefully.

"We don't want him to come out of this like a vegetable."

"Why not?"

"Better if he just has a memory gap. If it looks like he had a stroke, they might take him to the hospital and find something...off."

"Then what do we do instead?"

"Blast his hippocampus."

"Which is?"

"One of the areas of the brain that governs short-term memory. The other is the subiculum, which is next to it, but that's only for *very* short term."

He knew that they didn't have time for a medical-school lecture, but he sent her a picture of the brain, showing her the hippocampi, which were actually two horseshoe-shaped structures, one in the left-brain hemisphere and the other in the right.

"It takes in memories and sends them out to the appropriate part of the cerebral hemisphere where they are retrieved when necessary."

He knew she was studying the picture he'd sent.

The hippocampus. It's kind of at the bottom.

Yeah. He pulled at the limp body of the unconscious man, arranging him so that his knees were under him, his butt was in the air, and the back of his head was facing upward at an angle.

He didn't have to tell Elizabeth to give him power. She simply did it, and he felt it gathering inside himself—before he directed a thin stream of lightning at the back of the man's head. The guy's body jerked, and he fell over on his side.

Did that do it? Elizabeth asked.

Let's hope so. And there's one more thing we'd better do.

He picked up the gun, wiped it off with his shirttail, and put it into the man's hand.

Elizabeth tugged at Matt's arm. *Come on. Let's make tracks.*

Right.

They both headed back the way they'd come, making a wide circle around the man they'd left lying on the ground.

When they reached their car, he wanted to stop and pull her close, but he knew that the first thing they had to do was get away—before more of Lang's thugs came after them.

They both got into the car, and Matt drove off, thankful that nobody was shooting at them.

I'm hoping life isn't going to be a series of narrow escapes, she whispered in his mind.

We'll be a lot safer when Lang is out of the picture.

Chapter Eleven

Tony Verrazano rolled to his back trying to figure out where he was and what had happened to him.

He was outside. Yeah. He'd been on patrol at The Mansion.

But now he was lying on the hard ground with his head aching like a son of a bitch. His gun was in his hand, and he didn't remember drawing it. In fact, he couldn't call up any memories from the past few minutes.

How had he gotten here?

He struggled to pull anything recent into his mind, but nothing would come to him. In a panic, he sat up too quickly and winced at the stab of pain. After checking the safety on the gun, he stuffed it into his shoulder holster, then pulled up his knees and clasped his hands around his legs. Pressing his cheek to his knees, he ordered himself not to start shaking.

Something frightening had happened, and he didn't know what it was. Worse, he didn't even know how he'd gotten here. Yeah, he'd thought that before, hadn't he?

Still clenching his hands around his legs—he carefully went back to the last thing he did remember. He'd had a meal in the kitchen of the whorehouse where Lang kept the girls he'd imported from Eastern Europe. Then he'd gone out on patrol.

He'd been walking the ground, and something must have happened to him.

But what?

Had he seen something in the woods? Gone in here to
have a look? And then what?

Nothing like this had ever happened to him before, and
he struggled to tamp down the fear coursing through him.

Should he tell someone? What if an intruder had invaded
the property? Like the woman who had been here a week
ago. She was still on the loose, and the boss had ordered all
the guards to be extravigilant.

But he didn't think she was here now. Or at least he didn't
want it to be true. He got up and brushed off his clothing,
feeling a lot of dirt on the back of his pants, like he'd been
dragged into the trees. Could that be true?

Fear trickled down the back of his spine as he scrambled to come up with an alternative scenario. Maybe he'd
been investigating something in the woods, tripped over a
tree root in the dark, fallen down, hit his head and knocked
himself out.

Clumsy of him.

Well, he wasn't going to say anything about it and risk
getting fired from what he considered a very good job.

"NOW WHAT?" ELIZABETH asked as they put distance between
themselves and The Mansion.

"We shut the place down."

"I hate the idea of letting that house of horrors operate
for even the rest of today, but there's another reason we can't
just go to the police. Those women are in the U.S. illegally.
Probably they'll all be deported if we just call the cops."

"Yeah, even if they were brought here under false pre-
tenses, they could be caught in the system."

She sighed. "I wish I knew more about it. I don't want
to get them deported because I'm trying to help them." She
thought for a moment. "Maybe my best bet is going back to
Sabrina and seeing if there's some way her friends in Baltimore can shelter them."

He made a rough sound. "We're getting ourselves in deeper every time we turn around."

"I know. But I want those women out of there—then to find a way to destroy Lang's whole operation."

"That's a tall order. How long has he been in business?"

"I don't know exactly." She gave him a pleading look. "I realize this whole thing is a mess, but I want to see it through. Not just for me. Polly died because I was stalking Lang."

Relief flooded through her when he said, "Okay."

"I think we have to go find Sabrina."

He tightened his hands on the wheel.

She put her fingers on his arm, and she knew she didn't have to speak out loud for him to pick up what was in her mind. He turned off onto a two-lane road and slowed, finding a clearing where he could pull off the blacktop.

"You want to talk about how we're going to work it when we go back to the house?" he asked.

"Yes."

"What was your original plan?"

She flung her arm in frustration. "I wish I knew. Probably I hadn't come up with anything definite, which was why I hadn't acted."

"But you're thinking about something that might help."

She grinned. "You read me so well."

When he'd cut the engine, she unbuckled her seat belt and leaned toward him. Reaching for her, he pulled her close. They clung together, both of them thankful that they'd gotten away from The Mansion.

She pulled away so she could look at him. *What if we have a technique we can use?*

He knew she was thinking about a book she'd read— about a girl whose parents had been part of a government drug experiment in college. The people who survived came away with superpowers. For example, the girl's father had been able to influence the actions of others.

Did you read it? she asked.

Yes. It's by Stephen King.

In the book, the father called his power "giving people a push"—influencing their actions and perceptions.

And you think we can do that? Isn't that a little grandiose? he asked.

We won't know until we try it.

"We'd have to practice to make sure we could do it," he said.

"Of course."

"Who do we practice on?"

"I don't know yet."

He switched topics and asked, "Do you know the part of Baltimore where you met with Sabrina?"

"Yes. I think that's where I was going when I crashed my car." She gave him directions, and they drove back to the city.

"But you don't know exactly where to find Sabrina," he said as they got closer to the right part of town.

"I think I only knew her through Wendy—the woman who adopted a child and was one of my clients."

"Then we'll start there."

They drove to a neighborhood of typical Baltimore row houses, some with brick fronts and some faced with a man-made material that was supposed to resemble stone but looked more like something from a kid's construction set. Elizabeth had always wondered why anyone would want to put that stuff on a home.

"You know which house?" he asked.

"No. But I think I'll recognize it when I see it."

He drove up and down several blocks, and she scanned the facades, looking for some kind of clue.

Finally she saw a house with a planter full of geraniums beside the marble steps. "That's it!"

Matt found a parking space around the corner, and they walked back, then climbed the steps.

After ringing the bell, Elizabeth waited with her heart pounding because she didn't know what the woman inside looked like, but she was pretty sure she'd recognize her when she saw her.

The door opened, and Wendy stood on the other side of the storm door, an expression on her face that was a mixture of astonishment and anger.

"You said you'd come back days ago," she accused. "Where have you been? We've been waiting and worrying. I called social services, and they said you had…disappeared."

Elizabeth swallowed hard. "I'm sorry. Can we come in?"

Wendy looked like she was about to refuse.

Matt pressed his shoulder to Elizabeth's, and she suddenly knew that he was going to use the technique they'd discussed. *Don't turn Elizabeth away. She had a good reason for not coming.*

Elizabeth fought to keep her gaze on Wendy. They'd only speculated about trying this, and Matt doing it now had taken her completely by surprise. But had it worked? Especially since she hadn't even thought about giving him extra power.

"Is there a good reason why you didn't come back?" Wendy asked.

"She was in the hospital. I'm her doctor."

"Oh, I'm sorry," Wendy said. "You'd better come in."

They both stepped directly into a small living room with a bay window that looked onto the street. The room was cluttered with toys. When Wendy knelt to sweep some blocks into a pile, Elizabeth bent down also to help her, remembering the little girl who was so lucky to be living here.

"How's Olivia?" she asked.

"She's doing great. She's already in bed."

Elizabeth picked up a floppy stuffed rabbit from the sofa and stroked it. "I remember this room," she said.

"What do you mean?" Wendy asked.

"I had amnesia. That's why I didn't come back. Matt—Dr. Delano is helping me recover my memories."

"Oh, you poor thing," Wendy said. "Where are my manners? Please sit down."

Elizabeth and Matt sat together on the couch. Wendy looked at Matt, then Elizabeth, then back again. "You look more like her lover than her doctor."

Elizabeth flushed at the directness of the statement.

"We've gotten to know each other pretty well," Matt said. "Elizabeth was on the way here, to your meeting, when she was in an automobile accident."

"I didn't know."

"She was banged up, but the main problem was the amnesia. It took a while for us to put you and your friend Sabrina back into the picture."

Wendy nodded.

"We've been working on her memories, and she finally recalled enough to come here."

Again Wendy nodded cautiously.

"But there are things we can't piece together."

"Like what?"

"Sabrina said that friends of hers are being held at a house owned by...."

Wendy glanced toward the door, like she expected thugs to come charging in. "Derek Lang," she whispered.

"Yes. I didn't know how much I'd told you," Elizabeth said.

"A lot of it. Not everything."

"We need to talk to Sabrina."

Once again, they met resistance.

"I don't know," Wendy said. "It was hard enough for her to come here the first time. That Lang man is dangerous."

"Believe me, I know," Elizabeth murmured as she gripped the floppy rabbit she was still holding.

Beside her, Elizabeth heard Matt's silent suggestion. *Why don't we try again to influence her?*

All right.

She looked at Wendy. "I'm really sorry that I couldn't get back here sooner. Just now, Matt and I went out to the property and confirmed that the women are there. We need Sabrina's help to get them somewhere safe."

"You mean to the shelter where she is now?"

"Yes." Elizabeth had forgotten that Sabrina had hooked up with a secret welfare organization that was willing to take in illegal aliens. Thankful that problem had been solved, she silently urged Wendy, *Get up and call Sabrina. Tell her that I've come back, that I was in an accident, that I had amnesia and couldn't make it here sooner.*

She felt Matt adding power to help her project the unspoken message. Her pulse was pounding as she waited to find out what would happen. After a few seconds, she saw Wendy's face change.

"I guess it's not your fault that you didn't meet up with us."

This time it was Matt who sent the message. As soon as she heard it, Elizabeth sent him power to help project the suggestion.

Yes, that's right. Tell Sabrina to come right over. Tell her we need to speak to her.

Wendy stood up. "Let me go phone her."

"Thank you," Elizabeth answered. *We got her to change her mind,* she said to Matt.

But we don't know how effective we were. All we know is what she did. She could have made the decision on her own.

But she was reluctant to even let us come in before you... pushed her.

We'll see.

HAROLD GODDARD HADN'T forgotten about Matthew Delano. He had a service checking for any mention of the man's name—in print or on the internet—and so far it was like the doctor had disappeared off the face of the earth. Harold would have liked to think that no news was good news. In this case, he couldn't convince himself it was true.

So he kept checking and waiting for the other shoe to drop. Like what was going on with the woman named Jane Doe? Who was she really? He had a pretty good idea. Not her specific name. But he wouldn't be at all surprised to find out that her mother had been treated at the Solomon Clinic.

There was no proof of that yet, but he was willing to bet there would be.

And if there was one thing Harold didn't like, it was losing control of a situation. He'd deliberately thrown other couples together so he could watch what happened. Now he was pretty sure two others had gotten together on their own, and there was no telling where they were or what they would do. But he had the feeling he'd better be prepared for trouble.

Chapter Twelve

Matt and Elizabeth sat tensely on the sofa, waiting for Wendy to return. Elizabeth wanted to get up and follow her down the hall, but she suspected that the woman had deliberately left the room to give herself some privacy.

Too bad we can't amplify hearing, Matt murmured inside her head.

She answered with a small nod.

Their tension mounted with every minute Wendy was away, and Elizabeth started imagining all sorts of scenarios—like Derek Lang walking in the front door.

But finally Wendy returned with a cautious smile on her face.

"Sabrina's coming over."

Just then, a wailing cry from upstairs made Elizabeth jump.

"That's Olivia," Wendy said, "probably telling me that she needs her diaper changed."

She departed again, but this time Elizabeth felt relieved. They'd cleared one hurdle.

Ten minutes later Wendy was back, holding a one-year-old girl.

"Do you remember Miss Elizabeth?" she asked.

The little girl pointed to Elizabeth. When her mother set her down on the floor, she crawled toward the sofa and pulled herself up, grabbing on to Elizabeth's knee to steady herself.

"I'll be right back with a bottle," her mother said.

Elizabeth offered the little girl the bunny, and she snatched it away, hugging it.

This was familiar and bringing back more memories. She remembered that Wendy was a good mother—and willing to help the women who'd ended up in Derek Lang's clutches.

When Wendy returned, she unfolded the playpen by the window and set her daughter inside.

Olivia lay on her back, kicking her feet in the air as she held the bottle and sucked. Elizabeth watched the baby, thinking how sweet she was. But was she bringing danger to this family just by being in this house?

Lang doesn't know we're here, Matt said, and Elizabeth knew he'd caught the drift of her thoughts.

We should get out as soon as possible.

When the back door opened, she jumped, but she relaxed when she saw Sabrina striding down the hall. She was a woman of medium height, with short blond hair and cautious eyes. She looked delicate, but obviously had inner strength—and the courage and determination to get herself out of a bad situation.

When she spoke, it was with the thick accent Elizabeth remembered. But the words were not what Elizabeth had expected to hear.

"Are you the woman who was staying with that nurse when she was murdered?"

Elizabeth sucked in a sharp breath. "How do you know about that?"

"It was all over the news. And Wendy said that you claimed you had amnesia."

"I didn't claim. It's true."

"You're not just saying it to get out of helping us?"

Beside her Elizabeth could feel Matt sending the newcomer soothing thoughts.

It's all right. You were expecting Elizabeth to help you. You were scared and angry when she didn't come back. But now she's here, and she's going to help you like she promised.

Elizabeth saw Sabrina relax fractionally.

"I'm sorry I left you in the lurch," Elizabeth said.

"But you were staying with that nurse?"

"Yes. Are you going to call the police and tell them where I am? If they drag me into the investigation of Polly's death, then I won't be able to help you get your friends away from Lang."

Sabrina answered with a small nod.

"Lang's men were chasing me the day I was supposed to meet you. That's why I crashed my car, hit my head and ended up with amnesia. I couldn't meet you because I didn't remember anything."

Sabrina struggled to hold back a sob. "I waited for hours."

"I'm so sorry."

"I thought you'd changed your mind. Or…or you were too scared to do it."

"No. I still wasn't sure how to get in there, but now I have a plan," she said.

She knew Matt caught her thoughts when his hand closed around her arm. "No," he said.

"Can you think of anything better?" she asked.

After long seconds she felt his acquiescence and looked back at Sabrina. "Matt's going to get in there by pretending to be a customer. And I'm going to slip in the back way and mingle with the women. While Matt keeps the men away, I'll get the women out."

"You wanted to shut down his operation," Sabrina pointed out.

Elizabeth nodded. "I don't know if we can go that far. But we can rescue the girls who are there. And after everybody's out, we can burn the house down. That will set him back while we figure out the next step."

Sabrina looked torn. "I want him in jail for what he's done to me and the others."

"I do too, but it might not be possible." She changed the subject. "And you have that secret welfare organization ready to take them in and hide them until they can get new identities?"

"Yes." She turned her gaze on Elizabeth. "Can we go get my friends tonight?"

"It's better if we have everything planned. You need to get the welfare group ready with transportation, and Matt and I need to rehearse our roles," she answered.

Sabrina's expression turned fierce. "You want me to get a rescue operation organized tomorrow. How do I know that you're not going to disappear again?"

Elizabeth felt her heart squeeze. "I can't absolutely guarantee what's going to happen tomorrow night," she said. "But Matt and I plan to be there."

It was the best she could do, and she let out a sigh of relief when Sabrina nodded. "Where are we going to meet? How are we going to do it?"

Elizabeth hadn't thought about all the details, and because this woman was pressing her, she felt like the room was closing in on her.

Matt gave Sabrina an angry look. "I know you're worried about your friends, and I know you're anxious to get them out of Lang's clutches, but Elizabeth has already been through a lot because she committed herself to helping them. She's almost gotten killed more than once."

As he spoke aloud, Elizabeth knew he was sending Sabrina a soundless message. *Don't lean on Elizabeth. She's doing everything she can. She'll be ready tomorrow night. All you have to do is have a van ready to take your friends away from The Mansion.*

She saw Sabrina take a breath and let it out. "I'm sorry," she whispered. "I know I'm not making this any easier for you."

"It's okay," Elizabeth managed to say, then cleared her throat. "I told you that I had a memory loss when I crashed my car and everything hasn't come back to me yet."

Sabrina nodded.

"I need to ask you some questions. You might have answered them before, but I don't remember some details."

"I'll answer what I can."

"There are men at The Mansion who act as guards, but who is it that greets guests?"

"Mrs. Vivian."

"Where will she be?"

"Probably mingling with guests. She might also be near the door."

"I saw men eating and drinking."

"The Mansion orders a lot of prepared food. And the bar is always stocked."

"Is there any place the women aren't allowed to go?"

"They usually stay in the front."

"I'll be dressed like one of the women, but I'll probably have to come in through the kitchen."

"You could say you were getting a snack for a patron."

"Okay."

"How many bedrooms?" Matt asked.

"Eight."

"So each girl doesn't have her own room?"

"No. They bunk together, and use the nice bedrooms for entertaining guests."

"How many women will be there?" Matt asked.

"Twelve to fifteen."

They discussed more of the layout, before Elizabeth asked, "Will there be a problem getting the women to come with me?"

Sabrina's brow wrinkled as she considered the question. "Mention my name, and tell them I sent you to get them out."

"But there could be women you don't know."

And one of them could give her away, Elizabeth was thinking, but she didn't say it aloud because she didn't want to make it sound like she was coming up with objections.

"Are there guards inside the house?" she asked.

"In a guard station down the hall from the kitchen. They watch TV screens there."

The monitors for the cameras, Matt said.

Yes. Finally she knew that she'd gotten all the information she could before actually going into The Mansion.

"We should leave now," Matt said. "Can you give me the address of the shelter where you're going to take the women?"

Sabrina gave him an address several blocks away.

"We'll meet there at seven tomorrow night," he said, then stepped to the door and scanned the street. When he saw nothing suspicious, he ushered Elizabeth out.

They walked around the corner to his car, and she dropped into the passenger seat.

"Thank God I've got you," she whispered. "How did I ever think I could do this myself?"

"You had the courage to do it, but you didn't count on the lengths Lang would take to get you out of the way."

"Stupid of me."

"Of course not."

"I guess I didn't realize how ruthless he is."

"Because your background and training make you think about helping people—not hurting them."

When she started to speak, he leaned over and pressed his lips to hers. *But you do have me,* he said. *And we'll do it together.*

She wrapped her arms around his neck and leaned into the kiss.

They embraced for long moments, and she thought again how lucky she was to have found this man who was strong and determined—with the survival skills she lacked.

She knew he heard that when he smiled against her mouth. *I'm so open to you,* she silently murmured.

Likewise.

When she caught the thought in his mind, her breath stilled.

I love you.

Oh, Matt.

You had to know it was true.

But I never expected it—not ever in my life. I was always so alone.

And you know I was, too.

"I love you," she said aloud, knowing there was no need to speak. But she wanted to say the words because they were important to her.

She would have been overwhelmed by happiness, yet she couldn't allow herself that joy. Not yet. "We have a job to do," she whispered.

"And when we're finished, we can figure out what we're going to do for the rest of our lives."

"It will be easier if we can prove we had nothing to do with Polly's death," she said.

"I'm hoping that we can get evidence after we take care of Lang." He pulled away from the curb, heading for the motel.

"We still have to practice the skills we're going to need to pull off the rescue operation at The Mansion."

"And it's not going to be as easy as persuading two women who wanted to believe our story."

"I wouldn't exactly call Sabrina easy," she argued. "She was upset—and that made her angry with me."

"But I want to work on a person who isn't involved with us, and get him to do something totally against their best interests. Like in a restaurant."

She caught what was in his mind. "Is that fair?"

"This is love and war. And it's not like we're robbing a bank."

She understood his logic, but she still didn't like what he was planning.

When they returned to the vicinity of the motel, Matt drove around the restaurant area, looking for a place that was a cut above the fast-food restaurants with drive-in windows. He found a small Italian restaurant that didn't appear to be part of a chain.

"Do you want to do try and influence the counter men, or should I?" he asked.

"In this case, I think a guy will be more persuasive. If you can do it at all."

"Just give me some psychic energy."

They walked into the dining room, which had a central aisle and tables on either side. Framed scenes of Italy decorated the stuccoed walls. At the back was a counter with a menu above it. Two young men with short dark hair wearing white uniforms were behind the counter.

"Help you?" one of the men asked.

Matt studied the menu, and Elizabeth felt him getting ready to tell a whopper. "We have one of your certificates for a free meal," he said.

"We don't…" The man stopped in midsentence, looking confused.

Elizabeth could hear Matthew furiously projecting false information. *You believe me. I have a certificate that gives me a thirty-dollar free meal. It's a new offer, and I'm the first customer to cash it in.* He opened his wallet, took out a business card he'd gotten from a colleague and held it up. "See, here's my certificate." *And you don't need to take it away. You just need to look at it,* he added without saying anything aloud.

Elizabeth held her breath as she waited to find out what

would happen. Giving away food was so clearly against the restaurant's best interests that it seemed impossible that the guy would go along with Matt's suggestion.

The counterman eyed the card and nodded. "I am not familiar with it, but I guess it's okay—since you got this thing."

She could feel Matt relax a little as he turned to her. "What do you want, honey?"

She looked at the food that had already been prepared. "A calzone would be good."

"Make it two," Matt said. "And add a couple of sodas."

While the man was packing up the order, Matt made a silent suggestion. *We haven't spent near thirty dollars. Why don't you suggest that we take a couple cannolis?*

His audacity took Elizabeth's breath away, but she stood without speaking beside him, waiting to see if it worked.

"You haven't used the whole thirty dollars. How about two cannolis for dessert?" the counterman asked.

"Great idea," Matt agreed.

Elizabeth shot him a look as she waited for the man to come to his senses, but he cheerfully packed up the food and drinks and handed over the bag.

"Thanks," Matt said as they strolled out.

Elizabeth was in more of a hurry and had to keep herself from running to the car.

Once inside, she breathed out a deep sigh. "I guess if we ran out of money, we could work as con artists."

"It's only a temporary necessity—I hope. I mean until we get out from under the Lang problem and clear our names."

As they drove back to the motel, she could hear ideas flashing in Matt's mind. He was thinking about the next evening's raid on The Mansion.

But as soon as they entered the room and closed the door, he set the food down on the table and reached for her.

She came into his arms with a small sob.

"I'm sorry. I know you hate all this. You don't like stealing food, and you don't like the plans I'm making."

"I'd like to forget about them right now," she said.

He lowered his mouth to hers for a kiss that told her that he'd been wanting to be alone with her for hours.

She wiped everything from her mind but the feel of him, the taste, the emotions running wild between them. And when he pulled back the spread and took her down to the surface of the bed, she held on to him, then rolled far enough away so that she could tear off her slacks and panties.

He was doing something similar, only his pants didn't come all the way off. She pushed the sides of the zipper away and pulled his briefs down, freeing his erection. With his legs trapped, they didn't have many options. She straddled him, bringing him inside her before she began to move in a frantic rhythm that brought them both to climax almost immediately.

She collapsed on top of him, and his arms came up to fold her close.

As they clung together, he whispered, "It's going to be all right."

"We'll be walking into danger."

He asked the question she'd asked before. "Can you think of a better plan?"

Of course she couldn't. She hadn't been able to do that in the first place. And now the moment of reckoning was coming all too fast.

"We should eat before the food gets cold."

"Eat our ill-gotten gains?"

"Uh-huh."

"We should pay for it."

"We'll send the restaurant some money—when this is all over and we have access to our bank accounts."

"If it's ever all over." She gave him a fierce look. Tomorrow they were going to do their damnedest to take care of Lang's operation.

"Then on to the next problem," he said. They both knew that was solving the puzzle of how they'd ended up with powers that had only become accessible when they'd touched each other.

Chapter Thirteen

Derek Lang balled his hands into fists, then ordered himself to relax. It seemed like Elizabeth Forester had dropped off the face of the earth. It could be that she'd cut her losses and cleared out of town, but he wouldn't bet on it.

When he'd figured out that she was poking into his business, he had started digging up everything he could about the nosy bitch. One thing he knew was that she was persistent. Once she got a notion in her head, she wasn't going to let it go. Which meant that he'd better be prepared for whatever she had in mind.

He called in Gary Southwell, noting the way the man fought to hide his case of nerves.

"Did you get a report from The Mansion?" Derek asked.

"Yes. Everything's normal out there, except one of the cameras malfunctioned."

"Why?"

"We don't know."

"There's no chance someone could have tampered with it?"

"Not unless they climbed up on the roof."

"Who was on duty at the time?"

Southwell named several men, including Tony Verrazano.

"Any of them report anything unusual?"

"No, sir."

"Well, I want everyone extra-alert."

ELIZABETH AND MATT spent the day preparing for their invasion of The Mansion. After breakfast they both went to a local department store where Elizabeth bought a negligee like the ones she'd seen the women wearing. None of them had been wearing underwear. But because she hated the idea of walking around in a gown so revealing, she also purchased a chemise she could wear underneath.

Matt bought a sport coat and slacks on sale, an outfit that would make him look like the bordello's upscale patrons.

"We'd better stop at a drugstore," she said when they were finished with the clothes shopping. "I need some cosmetics, or I'm going to look out of place in there."

She'd already bought gray eye shadow and lipstick. She added foundation, eyeliner, blusher and mascara, going for products that weren't too expensive and hoping she'd be able to apply them artfully.

She and Matt brought lunch back to the motel room and spent the next few hours discussing various scenarios, but it was clear they could only go so far with the plans. Neither one of them knew exactly what was going to happen when they arrived at the bordello, and all they could do was outline several contingencies—which basically involved Matt keeping the management busy at the front of the house while she got the women out the back.

"How are you going to get away?" she asked.

"The same way I got in."

"You may need me to reinforce the messages you're sending. I can…"

He gave her a grim look. "Once you get the women out of there, you will not go back in."

She knew she had to agree, and she worked hard to keep him from realizing that she might not be able to keep her word.

"Get some sleep," he told her as she paced the motel room.

"I don't know if I can."

He closed the drapes, then lay down in the bed with her, cradling her in his arms.

They were both too keyed up to sleep, but it was a comfort to have him hold her.

Finally it was time to start getting ready.

"We should eat. I'll get more burgers and shakes."

"This isn't exactly a healthy diet."

"But it will have to do for now."

When he came back with the food, Elizabeth could barely choke any down. Finally she gave up, changed into the chemise and gown she'd bought and went into the bathroom to start playing with the cosmetics.

She began with foundation, then went on to lipstick, eyeliner, blusher and eye shadow. Standing back, she studied the effect, astonished at how different she looked. Then she finished it off with two applications of mascara.

When she came out, Matt did a double take.

"Wow."

"You like the effect?"

"You know I do." He eyed the gown. "I guess you fixed it so you can't see through it."

"I hope so."

She slipped her feet into mules, then reached for the light raincoat she'd bought.

Glad it was already getting dark, she crossed to the car and got in. And then they were on their way to the rendezvous spot.

When they arrived, Sabrina was pacing back and forth, looking anxious. As they pulled up, she visibly relaxed.

"I wasn't sure you'd come."

"I understand, but I had no intention of backing out," Elizabeth answered.

Sabrina introduced them to a woman named Brenda who worked at the shelter.

"Thank you for doing this," she said. "We can give them a

safe harbor once they come to us, but we're an underground organization, and we can't call attention to ourselves."

"I know that," Elizabeth answered. "But we'll get them to safety."

Brenda nodded, and Elizabeth wondered if the woman thought she could really pull this off.

As it turned out, Brenda was part of the operation. She would drive the van, and Sabrina would come along to help calm the women and keep order.

Matt would have to go in his own car because he'd be arriving at the front door like any normal customer.

She saw the tension on his face and knew he was worried about her. "I'll be okay."

"Just be careful." He turned to Sabrina. "Can you give the names of some of the men who…you were with in the house?"

"I don't know any of their last names."

"Give me some first names."

"There was Harry. Another one was Martin."

"Okay. I can use that. And you said the woman who runs the place is Mrs. Vivian."

"Yes."

"Then we're all set," he said, projecting confidence. He turned back to Elizabeth. "See you soon."

She gave him a fierce hug before climbing into the van. She could still feel his worry as Brenda drove away, and she kept up the connection with him as long as she could. When it snapped off, she clenched her fists, feeling suddenly very alone. She had gotten used to reaching for his mind, and now the connection had been cut off. But she'd get it again, she told herself. He'd be following in his car, and he'd arrive twenty minutes after she did.

She refocused her attention on her current reality.

"Don't head straight for the house," she told Brenda. "Drive past, and I'll show you where to park."

She directed Brenda up a dirt road into the woods to the place she and Matt had used when they came to check out The Mansion.

"Do you want me to come with you?" Sabrina asked.

"I appreciate the offer," Elizabeth told her. "But I think you should stay at the edge of the woods. That way, I'll be alone and less conspicuous."

She saw relief flood Sabrina's features. Although she knew the other woman had been prepared to go in if necessary, she also knew that the worst experiences of her life had taken place in that house. And the idea of stepping back into The Mansion terrified her. Elizabeth also knew Sabrina would have done it if Elizabeth had asked.

They made their way through the darkened woods, using the lights from the house as a beacon and circling around so that they were opposite the kitchen door.

Elizabeth and Matt had discussed how to handle the cameras. They'd already disabled one, and doing it again might put the security staff on alert. They'd decided her best bet was to keep her head down and walk to the back door. She wouldn't be visible until she was close, and hopefully anyone watching would think one of the girls had just slipped outside for a minute.

She watched for the guards she and Matt had seen. Just after one walked across the lawn between her and house, she strode across the lawn and made it to the back stoop, where she stood shaking, waiting for someone to burst outside and grab her. After more than a minute had passed, she breathed out a little sigh.

She'd gotten this far without any problems, but now came the real test.

Cautiously she tiptoed to the window beside the back door and looked in. A man who was probably one of the security staff was in the kitchen helping himself to food from the refrigerator, and she waited with her heart pounding while he loaded a plate.

Don't sit down at the kitchen table, she told him over and over. *Take the food where you'll be more comfortable.*

Her breath was shallow as she waited to see what he would do. He stood in the kitchen for endless seconds, holding the plate, before finally walking out of the room with the food.

When he was gone, she remembered to breathe again. She wanted to get this over with, yet she was glad that she'd had a little more time before she had to go in there.

She turned the knob and pushed the door open, then stepped inside and quietly closed it behind her.

Taking a few steps forward, she looked for the back stairs that Sabrina had told her about. She also saw a short hallway and knew it led to the guard station. She didn't want to go there, but it had to be a priority.

"Get it over with," she ordered herself, then crossed to the hallway and tiptoed farther into the house. At the end of the hall, she could see a small room with monitors flickering. The man who'd gotten the food was sitting with his back to her, looking at screens showing various views of the grounds. The plate was on a table beside him. Apparently he'd left his post and hadn't been looking at the monitors when she'd crossed the lawn.

Gathering her power, she sent a beam of energy to the back of his head, holding it as long as she could, hoping she'd put him in a coma.

Because tying him up would be too suspicious, she left him there and headed back toward the steps. She paused at the top, getting her bearings.

From the shadows where she stood, she saw a middle-aged man and a young brunette woman step out of a bedroom, and she pressed herself against the wall. But the guy wasn't paying any attention to her. His attention was focused on his companion.

He gave her a familiar pat on the rear, then strode to the front steps. The brunette was achingly young looking, and Elizabeth could only imagine what the poor girl had been through since leaving her own country.

She stood staring after her customer, a resigned expression on her face, then glanced up as Elizabeth hurried toward her.

Her expression turned to one of surprise as she stared at the woman who had materialized in the hallway.

"Who are you? Are you new here? Did you come in with another shipment?" she asked in heavily accented English.

"No. I'm helping Sabrina. I'm a social worker from Baltimore, and I met her there. I told her I'd come back here for the rest of you."

The statement was met with astonishment. "We haven't seen Sabrina in months."

"She's fine."

"Truly?"

"Yes. She and I worked out a plan to get the rest of you away from this place."

Fear and uncertainty flooded the woman's face. "You can't get us out of the house. We're guarded."

"Sabrina got out. You can too," Elizabeth answered, silently projecting the idea that escape from this hellhole was possible. "What's your name?"

"Maria."

"I'm Elizabeth."

"You're sure we can get away? And they won't kill us?" she asked in a shaky voice, her accent thickening with her mixed emotions.

"Yes. Do you know how many…guests are in the house?"

"Not many. It's still early."

"I need your help, Maria," Elizabeth said, projecting calm and certainty. "We need to get the other girls together."

Hope warred with fear on the woman's face. "Yes, all right. But some of them are downstairs, waiting for patrons."

"Get the ones up here together," Elizabeth said, knowing that they would have to wait for Matt to arrive to complete the mission.

MATT PULLED INTO the long drive and headed for the parking spaces at the front of The Mansion. There were only a couple cars already on site, and he was glad there wouldn't be too many civilians to deal with.

He got out, straightened his jacket and walked confidently to the front door, where he rang the bell.

After a few seconds, a nice-looking middle-aged woman opened the door. She was the woman he'd seen through the window when they were here the day before. Tonight she was wearing a beaded black dress and stylish pumps. She tipped her head to the side as she stared at him, obviously wondering who he was and how he'd gotten there.

"May I help you?"

"Mrs. Vivian?"

"Yes," she answered cautiously.

"I'm a friend of Harry's. He highly recommended this place if I wanted some relaxation."

"Harry who?"

"Harry," he repeated as he projected silent messages toward her. *I'm a friend of Harry. You trust Harry, and you trust me. You're so happy to have a new customer. You're glad Harry referred me. Let me in.*

He saw Mrs. Vivian wavering and poured on the reassuring messages.

"Come in," she finally said.

He stepped into the front hall, which was furnished with expensive-looking antiques. The hostess led him from there into an opulently furnished parlor. The rug on the polished wood floor was a palace-sized Oriental. The tables and chests were classic period pieces, and the sofas and chairs were comfortably modern.

"Harry told you our fees?" Mrs. Vivian murmured.

"Yes."

"You pay in advance."

"That's fine."

Five young women wearing negligees much like the one Elizabeth had donned were standing at one side of the room. They had been in various relaxed poses. When they saw him, they straightened, all of them arching their backs so that their breasts were thrust toward him.

So how did guys behave when they got here? Did they take some time to relax, or did they get right to business? Too bad he didn't have any experience with high-class bordellos. Or sex for hire.

He walked toward them, pretending he was trying to decide which one he wanted.

Unfortunately he couldn't just take all of them upstairs with him and disappear out the back way.

"What are your names?" he asked, stalling for time until he knew Elizabeth had gotten the first group out of the house.

They answered in turn, their English much like Sabrina's.

"Blossom."

"Daphne."

"Tara."

"Belinda."

"Jasmine."

"And what are you particularly good at?"

All of them flushed, but they began to name various sexual activities.

UPSTAIRS ELIZABETH WAITED in the hall. She'd heard the doorbell ring, and she prayed that Matt had arrived.

When she reached for his mind, she found him and breathed out a sigh of relief.

Everything okay? he asked.

Yes. I'm going to take a bunch of women down the back stairs and into the kitchen. If the coast is clear, I'll send them to Sabrina. She's waiting at the edge of the woods.

There are five women down here. I'll see if I can get them to the back of the house.

She broke off the voiceless conversation with Matt as Maria hurried back with six more women. Some looked frightened. Others doubtful.

"Everything's going to be all right. We'll go down the back stairs. The way I came up," Elizabeth said.

She debated whether to get them dressed in something more suitable for the outside, then decided that the better alternative was to get them away from the house as quickly as possible.

She put a finger to her lips in the universal symbol for quiet, then led the way down the stairs, pausing at the bottom to make sure that none of the guards had come back to get a snack.

The coast was clear, and she motioned for the others to follow.

The women peered around fearfully as they stepped into the kitchen, all of them looking like they expected a slave master to materialize out of nowhere and punish them for being downstairs.

It's all right. Everything's all right. You're perfectly safe. You're going to get away from here, Elizabeth kept assuring them. At the back door, she repeated the procedure she'd used when she arrived, waiting for a guard to pass. As soon as he had disappeared around the corner of the house, she opened the door and pointed toward the section of trees straight back from the door.

"Nobody is watching the video monitors. Sabrina is over there waiting for you. Go to her. She'll get you to the van."

The first woman cautiously stepped outside and started

across the lawn. The rest followed, and Elizabeth watched them go. She breathed out a small sigh as she saw them make it to the shelter of the trees. From the shadows Sabrina waved, and Elizabeth waved back.

Now they just had to get the women out of the parlor, and they'd be home free.

She turned and made her way toward the front of the house and stopped short when she saw Matt.

I'm here, she said.

I'm going to tell Mrs. Vivian that I'd like to take this group of women into the kitchen.

Will that work?

She's been completely cooperative so far.

But that could be problematic.

We'll see.

She heard Matt switch his mental attention to the hostess.

I love cooking. I'm taking the girls into the kitchen for some treats.

"What?" the woman said aloud.

"We're just going back to the kitchen to whip up some brownies," Matt said, madly projecting the message to Mrs. Vivian that what he was doing was perfectly normal.

"Come on," he said to the women.

None of them moved.

You get them to come with you out the back door. I'll keep Mrs. Vivian in line until you tell me they've all made it to the woods.

They had just started across the room when Matt heard a car pull up in the parking area.

Damn. It would have been better if they hadn't had to deal with another guest.

As that thought flickered through Matt's mind, the front door opened.

Another guest?

It was apparently someone so sure of his welcome here

that he didn't need to ring the bell or knock. The footsteps in the hall gave Matt a bad feeling.

He turned to see a tall, broad-shouldered man who appeared to be in his late forties stride into the room with the confidence of someone who knew no one was going to challenge him.

He stopped short when he saw Elizabeth, and a smile spread across his face.

Chapter Fourteen

"So good of you to show up here," Derek Lang said as he and the man next to him both drew handguns. The other man pointed his weapon at Matt. Lang covered Elizabeth.

Elizabeth's body went cold. This was the thug she'd been running from for more than a week, and she'd just put herself into his clutches.

Above the buzzing in her brain, she heard Matt switch his attention to Lang.

It's all right. Everything's okay. We're not doing any harm. We're going to walk out of here with these girls. And you're glad to see them go. None of them was working out, anyway.

Elizabeth knew she should add her power to Matt's mental assault, but for long moments, she simply couldn't manage it. It was all she could do to lock her knees and keep standing there in front of the man who had been repeatedly trying to kill her.

And apparently Matt's mental suggestion wasn't having any effect on Lang.

Help me, he shouted in her mind

She pulled herself together and added her strength to Matt's, but Lang's will must be strong. He acted like he hadn't heard the powerful suggestions they were now both aiming at him, and she realized that they should have simply zapped him instead of trying to convince him of something so against his best interests.

But it was already too late. He slammed Elizabeth against the wall, making her head ring as he fixed her with a murderous look. "You're going to be sorry that you ever got involved in my business."

He kept his hand on Elizabeth as he turned to the tough-looking man standing next to him. "Southwell, lock them in the basement."

He stopped and thought about the order. "No, wait. There's something strange about these two. They keep getting away, and I can't explain why. I want them separated. Leave Ms. Forester with me up here, and put Dr. Delano in the basement."

Elizabeth was still trying to clear her head, and she understood why Matt hadn't zapped Lang. The man was holding on to her, and if Matt hit him, he'd hit her, too.

Southwell flicked the gun at Matt. "Come on, let's go."

Elizabeth wanted to scream, but she wasn't going to show Lang that she was terrified. She watched the minion hustle Matt out of her sight.

It's okay. Everything's going to be okay. Matt sent her the reassurance over and over, but she didn't believe it. How could they possibly get out of this?

When Southwell and Matt were out of sight, Lang looked toward Mrs. Vivian, who was watching the scene wide-eyed.

"How did that guy get in here?"

"He said he was a friend of Harry."

"Harry who?"

"I...don't know."

Lang snorted. "We'll discuss that later. I want the girls upstairs out of the way. Elizabeth will stay here with me," he said, tightening his hand on her arm. "Bring me some rope."

"Yes, sir." Mrs. Vivian turned to the women. "You heard Mr. Lang. Go upstairs to your dormitory."

She followed the young women out of the room, leaving Elizabeth alone with Lang. He looked pleased with himself as he kept the gun on her and inclined his head toward a straight chair near the wall. "Sit down there."

With no other choice, Elizabeth sat, struggling to calm the pounding of her heart. She'd understood that sneaking into The Mansion was dangerous, but she hadn't anticipated that Lang was going to show up.

Mrs. Vivian was back all too quickly, holding a coil of rope.

"Tie her arms behind the chair back. Then tie her legs to the chair legs."

Don't do it. Don't tie me up, Elizabeth silently screamed, still fighting the fuzzy feeling in her head and trying desperately to project the message toward the woman who was standing meekly beside the chair.

When Mrs. Vivian hesitated, Lang's reaction was immediate and furious. "What are you waiting for? Tie her up, if you don't want me to shoot you."

The woman made a low sound and hurried in back of Elizabeth, pulled her arms back and began to wrap the rope around her wrists.

Don't make the bonds tight. Give my hands some circulation, Elizabeth said, not sure if that was going to do her any good. But maybe if the bonds were loose enough, she'd have a chance of getting free. Or maybe she'd get clearheaded enough to zap Lang, although she still couldn't risk it when he was holding the gun on her. And what good would that do if she was tied up?

THE HARD-FACED MAN named Southwell, who'd already tried to kill Elizabeth and Matt, marched Matt out of the room.

As soon as they were out of sight, Matt started to send his captor a message that he should let him go. Before he got out more than half a thought, the man raised his gun and brought the butt down on Matt's head.

He dropped to the floor, desperately trying to cling to consciousness.

"That's for all your tricky plays," the thug said, his tone understated. "You got me in a lot of trouble with the boss, and I don't much appreciate that. You're lucky I don't kill you now. But I think Mr. Lang wants to talk to you. I'm hoping he gives you to me when he's finished."

Matt heard the tirade through the fog in his brain.

"Get up."

When he was slow to comply, Southwell grabbed Matt's arm and dragged him toward the kitchen. He was aware of being pulled across the tile floor. They stopped as the guy opened a door. Then Matt was being dragged down the steps, his limp body thumping against the risers as they descended into the cold and dark room.

The guy reached the bottom, hoisted Matt onto his shoulder and carried him across an open space to a small room. He tossed him inside like a sack of rice. Matt hit the floor and lay still.

Southwell crossed the room and kicked him in the ribs, sending a wave of agony through his side.

"You'll be damn sorry that you made the mistake of hooking up with Elizabeth Forester. I'll be back when the boss wants to have a crack at you."

The thug closed the door behind him, leaving Matt dizzy and disoriented on the cold floor.

IN ONLY A FEW MINUTES, Elizabeth was tied to the chair, but Mrs. Vivian had at least done what was requested. Elizabeth thought she had a little bit of wiggle room at her wrists, and maybe if she had some time alone, she could get away.

Lang walked over, studying her. "I see the little social worker looks more like a prostitute. The outfit becomes you. Maybe as part of your punishment, I can let my men have some fun with you."

Elizabeth fought not to react.

"You know, the way your hands are tied thrusts your breasts toward me." When he reached down and cupped one in his hand, she tried to cringe away, but the chair and the ropes stopped her.

He pinched her nipple hard, and she couldn't hold back a gasp.

"What possessed you to get involved in my affairs?" he asked in a conversational voice.

She forced herself to raise her head and looked at him. "I couldn't leave those poor women here against their will."

"You're a real angel of mercy."

She didn't bother with a retort.

"How did you learn about this place?" he asked.

Thinking she'd made a mistake by answering his first question, she pressed her lips together. No way was she going to tell him about Sabrina. Oh, Lord, she thought suddenly. Sabrina was in the woods across the lawn, and the guards were still outside patrolling the grounds. Could she send Sabrina a message? Warn her?

All that was racing through her mind when Lang asked his question again.

"Where did you learn about my private business?"

When she didn't answer, he slapped her hard across the face.

In the basement room, Matt scooted backward so that he was propped against the wall. It was almost pitch dark, and he could see nothing.

He tried to reach out to Elizabeth, but his brain was too fogged to make the connection.

Was she all right? What was Lang doing to her up there? The pictures in his mind terrified him. He had to get out of this room, but he had no idea how.

But first things first. Southwell had roughed him up, but

was there any serious damage? Quickly he began to take a physical inventory. His head hurt where the thug had clunked him, and he knew he was going to have bruises where he'd thumped against the stairs and been kicked in the ribs. But as far as he could tell, nothing was broken, and he had no internal injuries, thank God.

He stayed where he was for several minutes, then pushed himself to his feet and felt the surface behind him. It was a wall made of brick, because the house must have been built before the age of cinder-block construction. Next, he walked along the wall, turning a corner where new cinder block met the old brick, making him wonder if the room had been constructed as a cell. For what? To discipline women who didn't want to cooperate?

He grimaced as he thought about that but kept walking carefully and holding out his hands in front of him so that he wouldn't smack into anything.

When his shoulder brushed something different, he stopped. He'd reached the door where he'd been thrown in here. Positioning himself in front of it, he began to feel his way over the surface. It seemed to be made of wood, and when he thumped his fist against it, it felt very solid. Not one of those hollow-core jobs, yet somehow he had to get out of here.

If he could only see the room, he'd have a better idea of how to escape. But there was no light source except for a thin line at the bottom of the door, making him as good as blind.

In frustration he smashed his fist against the door. Then he realized he wasn't thinking straight at all. He wasn't going to break out of here in any conventional way, but he and Elizabeth had used bolts of energy to zap rocks and then the men coming after them. Couldn't he use that power to free himself?

He backed across the room and braced his shoulders

against the wall, then tried to send a bolt of power toward the door. All he got was a massive jolt of pain in his head.

He cursed aloud in the little room, then took several breaths, gritted his teeth and tried again.

UPSTAIRS, LANG BACKED away from Elizabeth and stared at her, studying her like a rat he'd cornered in the basement.

"You think you can keep from spilling your guts to me?" he asked.

When she said nothing, he shook his head. "What if I told you I was going to poke a knife into your eye? Would that help to loosen your tongue?"

Fear leaped inside her, but she kept her voice even. "If you were going to do that to me, I'd know you were planning to kill me. And what would be the advantage of telling you anything?"

"There are many ways to die, some a lot more painful than others," he answered.

From the side of the room, Mrs. Vivian was watching and listened to the unfolding scene with a sick look on her face. Elizabeth would bet that she'd never anticipated anything like this when she had signed up to run Lang's bordello.

Elizabeth switched her attention away from the woman when she saw movement in the doorway in back of Lang. Afraid it was the henchman coming back, she braced herself.

But it wasn't the man who had taken Matt down to the basement. It was the guy they'd called Baldy, whom they had encountered outside when they had scoped out the place a few days ago. The man Matt had disabled with a jolt of energy to his brain.

DOWN IN THE basement room, Matt marshaled his energy. He hadn't been able to blast the door, and that wasn't an acceptable outcome. He had to get out of here because Lang had Elizabeth upstairs, and the man had already been angry with her. Now that he had her in his clutches, there was no telling what he would do.

Matt clenched his fists, gathering his will, putting everything into his effort to escape. Coldly he told himself there was no room for failure as he aimed a blast of power at the lock on the door. This time he felt the mental energy shoot out of his mind and hit the door with such force that he would have been knocked backward if he hadn't already been standing with his shoulders against the brick wall. The door rocked on its hinges but stayed in place. Matt redoubled his efforts, keeping up the stream of power, praying that it was enough to get him out of here.

The lock finally gave, and the door burst open, slamming against the outer wall.

For a moment Matt couldn't move. The effort had taken so much out of him that he could barely stay on his feet, but he knew that he had to get to Elizabeth. Finally he summoned enough energy to stagger out of the room. As he passed through the doorway, he felt a jolt of heat and realized that the door frame was smoldering.

In the outer part of the basement, he crossed the floor as quickly as he could, heading for the stairs. Looking back, he saw that the door frame was now on fire, and the flames were creeping toward the joists of the floor above.

He and Elizabeth had talked to Sabrina about burning down the house, but not while they were still in it.

Chapter Fifteen

Elizabeth saw that Baldy's face was strained, and she had the feeling he hadn't been doing so well since their encounter outside The Mansion.

She and Matt hadn't been able to influence Lang's actions, but this guy was another matter.

She focused on him, using every ounce of power she possessed to send him a message.

The man in front of you is an enemy invader. You have to disable him. He's holding me captive. You have to disable him so I can get away.

She watched Baldy's visage. Confusion and doubt chased themselves across his features as he tried to figure out what was true and what wasn't.

Lang saw that she was staring at someone behind him and turned.

Enemy. He's an enemy, Elizabeth silently screamed. *Disable him.*

Baldy blinked.

"Tony, what are you doing here? Is your shift over?"

So his name was Tony.

His mouth opened and closed as he stared at his boss, puzzlement on his face.

Elizabeth frantically continued to send him false information.

The man in front of you is an enemy. He's here to attack The Mansion. Disable him.

Tony pulled out a gun and pointed it at Lang.

"What are you doing, you fool?" the crime boss shouted.

In the next moment, Tony pulled the trigger and Lang went down.

From in back of the shooter, another man appeared, and this time it was the guy named Southwell who had taken Matt away.

"Watch out," Elizabeth shouted at Tony. "There's another invader."

The man whirled, just as Southwell pulled the trigger of his own gun.

Tony went down, but Southwell jumped back. And as Elizabeth stared at the scene, she caught the scent of smoke wafting toward her. It could be a malfunctioning fireplace, but she didn't think so.

She glanced at Mrs. Vivian and saw the woman's eyes were wide with panic. "The house is on fire. Help me get untied."

The woman didn't move.

Help me! You have to help me!

Matt stared at the flames, knowing he didn't have a lot of time now. As he hurried to the steps, he heard the sound of gunfire upstairs.

Oh, Lord, had Lang shot Elizabeth?

Matt had put his foot on the first riser when he saw a figure at the top. It was Southwell, the man who had locked him in the cell down here—no doubt coming to finish him off. But he was staring into darkness, and apparently couldn't see what had happened in his absence.

Matt jumped to the side, waiting for the man to come down. When he reached the basement, Southwell started for the cell, then stopped short when he apparently spotted the burning door frame. Matt leaped on his back, taking him down to the cement floor.

Southwell grunted, struggling, and Matt knew he had to finish this quickly. He was in bad shape, and there was no way he could match this guy in a physical fight.

Smoke was filling the basement now, and both men began to cough.

The thug flipped Matt over and tried to bring his gun hand up.

Mustering every shred of power he had left, Matt tried to send a thunderbolt toward the guy, but it was like a firecracker that failed to go off.

Just as the man yanked his arm free, he went rigid above Matt.

He looked up to see a woman at the top of the stairs. It was Elizabeth, and she'd apparently done what Matt couldn't—zapped Southwell.

Matt yanked the gun from the thug's limp hand and bashed him on the head with it, then bashed him again. Shoving himself up, Matt staggered toward the steps.

He and Elizabeth met in the middle, clasping each other tightly.

"Thank God you're all right," they both said at the same time.

Matt forced himself to ease away. "We need to get out of here. And the women, too."

"You're hurt," Elizabeth breathed as he wavered on his feet.

"I'm mobile," he answered, because he had to be.

Clinging to each other, they made it to the kitchen. Just as they stepped onto the tile floor, water started gushing down from the ceiling.

"The sprinkler system kicked in," Matt said. "Maybe it will put out the fire, but the place is still full of smoke."

"The girls are upstairs," Elizabeth told him.

"We can't leave them here," he answered. When he started up the back stairs, Elizabeth followed. There was no water on the stairs, but as soon as they got to the upper hall, water started pouring down on them again.

"They met you already. Tell them the situation," Matt said.

"Lang's dead," Elizabeth called when she reached the upper floor. "And the house is on fire. We have to get out of here."

For long seconds, nothing happened.

As Matt started down the hall, a door opened and one of the women stepped out, water pouring down on her and a lamp base in her raised hand. It was clear she intended to use it as a weapon. When she saw Matt's battered face, she drew in a quick breath.

"The house is on fire. We have to get out of here," Elizabeth repeated, sending that message to the woman in the doorway and hoping it was reaching the others who must be in there.

The door opened wider, and more faces peeked out.

"Come on," Elizabeth shouted. "Your friends who were up here are already out of the house. They're safe."

As she spoke, she heard a roaring noise behind her and saw flames shooting up the back stairs where there were no sprinklers.

Matt turned and saw the fire. "We have to get out the front door," he said.

Women soaked to the skin hurried out of the room, and Elizabeth ushered them to the stairs. At the bottom, they stopped to stare at the bodies on the living-room floor.

"The bad man," one of the girls confirmed.

"And one of those evil guards," another added.

Matt brought up the rear, herding the women away from the bodies and to the front door. Then from outside, Elizabeth heard the sound of gunfire and knew that the guards were out there—determined to keep everyone in the burning house.

Behind her, she heard Matt issuing hasty instructions.

"No," she gasped as she looked from him to the line of

three men who were about thirty yards away, all facing the door with weapons drawn.

"Can you think of anything else?" he asked, his voice grim.

Nothing came to her, but she still protested. "You're in no shape to do anything like that."

"I am if you help me."

In back of them, water poured down and smoke billowed, making everyone cough. They might all die of smoke inhalation if they didn't get out.

We couldn't influence Lang.

His will was too strong. These guys are just hired help.

"Here goes nothing," Matt muttered as he swiped a hand over his wet face, then stepped toward the door.

"This is Derek Lang. Cease fire," he called out. "I have to get these women out of here." He reinforced the words with a silent command, broadcasting the message to the guards outside, and Elizabeth did her best to help, lending him power.

For a long moment, nothing happened. Then someone called, "Mr. Lang?"

"Yes. We're coming out."

Elizabeth's heart was in her throat as Matt stepped out, still sending the voiceless message. She continued to help him, praying that the men outside would believe the illusion he was projecting—and that the women behind them wouldn't question what was going on.

Matt stepped out onto the porch, then turned and gestured to her and the others. "Come on."

At first, nobody moved. But then a crackling sound on the stairs behind them made them jump. Like the back stairs, the front ones were not protected by the sprinkler system and were burning.

Still projecting to the men outside, Matt walked down the porch steps, and the women followed, with Elizabeth ushering them along.

Then she saw something that made her catch her breath. Figures moved behind the line of men on the lawn. And as she watched, Sabrina and some of the other women sprang from the shadows, moving in unison. Each of them carried a club made from a tree branch. One of them brought the makeshift weapon down on the head of a guard who had kept them from escaping. Others clubbed them as they went down, whacking them on the backs and shoulders The men didn't have time to fire as they all succumbed.

Matt rushed forward, grabbing automatic weapons from one of the men and then another. Elizabeth snatched up the third gun.

"Get them to the van," Matt shouted as he stood and covered the women's escape. "You, too," he told Elizabeth.

This time she wasn't willing to go along with his plan. She waited with him.

When one of the guards started to get up, Matt shot at the ground in front of the man, and they all went still. She and Matt backed away. As they got to the trees, they turned and ran.

Elizabeth led the way to the van. As soon as they were all inside, Brenda gunned the engine, and the vehicle rocketed off.

The shelter had brought blankets in case the women needed them, and it was definitely true now. Matt, Elizabeth and the other women who had gotten showered wrapped themselves to keep warm.

They drove around to the road, and as they went past The Mansion's driveway, they could see that the sprinklers had put out most of the fire, but smoke still poured into the sky.

"I guess The Mansion's ruined," Elizabeth said.

"And Derek Lang is out of the picture," Matt added.

"One of his own men shot him," Elizabeth said, not explaining that she was the one who had made the voiceless suggestion. And she wasn't completely sure how she felt about that.

She knew Matt caught her thought as he slung his arm around her and pulled her close.

I left Southwell in the basement, he told her privately. *He probably didn't get out. What about Mrs. Vivian?*

I don't know, and I don't much care. If she's still alive, she's out of a job.

Elizabeth rested her head on Matt's shoulder, glad that they were both out of Lang's line of fire. Matt slipped his hand under her blanket and stroked up and down her arm, reassuring her as they drove away from the scene of what could have been a total disaster.

"You need medical attention," she whispered.

"Dr. Delano says I'm all right," he answered.

What did Southwell do to you?

Kicked me around a little.

He told her about being locked in the basement cell. And she tried to tone down the scene of being tied to the chair and threatened. But Matt caught the gist of what had happened.

The bastard.

He's dead.

And with the fire out, the cops will be able to figure out that one of Lang's own men killed him.

Elizabeth looked up to see the other passengers watching them.

"I didn't think you could do it," Sabrina said.

"Elizabeth wasn't going to let you down," Matt answered. "She was going to rescue you or die trying. And I think you all know it was a close call."

There were murmurs of agreement around the van.

"I think I forgot to say 'thank you,'" Sabrina whispered.

"I'm just sorry it took so long to get everyone out," Elizabeth answered.

They pulled up in back of the shelter, and the women poured out. They all went inside, and the director, a woman named Donna Martinson, came up to them.

"I can't thank you enough for what you did," she said.

Elizabeth looked down at the blanket and the wet flimsy gown she was wearing. "Actually, there is something you can do. I'd like to dry off and put on something more suitable," she said.

"Of course. We have clothing ready for the women. You can use the downstairs bathroom."

"I have my own things. I just need to get them."

She and Matt both went to his car, where he got out his computer and she got her suitcase. In the bathroom, she quickly took off the negligee and tossed it onto the floor, then put on a bra and panties before donning jeans, a T-shirt, socks and running shoes. When she was dressed, she stuffed the negligee into the trash can and jammed it down, then stood for a moment with her fists clenched. She'd been in Derek Lang's house of horrors for about an hour, but the women there had been through a much longer ordeal, although they hadn't been tied up and threatened with torture. At least she hoped not.

She stood for long moments, struggling for calm. She'd been through a lot of terrible experiences in the past few days, but the most recent one was the worst.

When she came out of the bathroom, Donna was waiting for her. "How are you feeling?" she asked.

"Better."

"Dr. Delano is using one of the offices," the director said, leading Elizabeth down a short hall.

"Thank you."

She went in and closed the door. Matt had also changed into the clothes from his bag in the trunk. He had been sitting at the desk with his laptop. He stood quickly, and she looked at the bruises on his face.

"How are you?" she asked.

"Fine."

She knew the answer was automatic as he came around the desk and took her in his arms.

He didn't have to ask how she was doing. She knew he was listening to her thoughts. And she was doing the same with him.

They clutched each other tight, both thankful that they had made it out of The Mansion.

I never would have gotten through this without you, she told him.

Yeah, well, I can't imagine...

He didn't finish the thought, but she knew what it was. And she felt the same. Neither one of them could imagine a life that didn't include the other.

"Are we going to be able to live our lives?" she asked. "I mean, the cops still want to talk to us about Polly."

"We'll make sure we can," he answered with conviction, and she wondered if that was simply wishful thinking.

He caught the question and answered. "I was just writing an email to the Baltimore County detective who was investigating Polly's death—a guy named Harrison. Unfortunately explaining what's been happening is a little tricky. But we lucked out with the sprinkler system. The house didn't burn up and destroy all the evidence."

He returned to his seat, and she pulled up a chair next to his, reading the message he'd started writing.

From Matthew Delano to Detective Thomas Harrison:
   You may be aware of a murder and fire in Harford County at a mansion that was being used by mob boss Derek Lang as a house of prostitution.

He paused and looked at Elizabeth as she kept reading.

An investigation of the scene will determine that Lang was shot by one of his own men, someone named...

"Tony," she supplied.

"No last name?"

"Not that Lang said."

"Okay."

She went back to reading.

Tony, who was shot in turn by another one of Lang's operatives, a man named Southwell, who subsequently ran into the basement. I also believe you will find, when you examine Southwell's gun, that it was the same weapon used to kill Polly Kramer, who was sheltering Elizabeth Forester, the woman known as Jane Doe when she was brought into Memorial Hospital suffering from amnesia.

He stopped and looked at her. "All right so far?"

"Yes."

As a social worker for the city of Baltimore, Elizabeth Forester had discovered a pattern of abuse involving Derek Lang. When he learned she was investigating him, he sent men to apprehend her. As they were pursuing her through the city, she was involved in a one-car accident. She was taken to Memorial Hospital suffering from amnesia. When she could not be identified, a nurse at the hospital, Polly Kramer, volunteered to take Elizabeth home.

I became involved in the case because I was the physician on call. Lang's men tracked Elizabeth down at Mrs. Kramer's house. Elizabeth was able to escape, but Mrs. Kramer was unfortunately killed by Lang's man, Southwell.

He stopped again. "Does that make sense?"

"Yes."

"Now comes the tricky part."

"Because there's no way we're going to betray Donna Martinson and the women we rescued," Elizabeth supplied.

Matt nodded.

Lang was trying to kill Elizabeth because, through her job as a social worker, she had discovered that he was forcing women into prostitution, and he wanted to keep her from acting on that information. We are confident that the results of the ballistics test will clear up the questions about Mrs. Kramer's murder.

He signed it Matthew Delano, MD.

"I guess we have to wait for a response before we can do anything else," he said.

"Do you think that will get us off the hook?" she asked.

"I hope so."

He continued silently. *The problem is that we can't give away the location of this safe house or the identities of the women.*

Yeah. That could be a deal breaker.

THEY DIDN'T HAVE long to wait for a reply. A demand came back pretty quickly that Matt and Elizabeth surrender themselves.

They politely declined. And the detective must have expedited the ballistics test, because it was only six hours later that they were given confirmation that the same gun had killed both Polly and Tony. Once that was established, Harrison asked to meet them at a neutral location.

"He could be lying to us," Elizabeth said. "On the TV shows, they don't have any compunction about saying whatever it takes to get people into custody—or to confess."

"Yeah, but you're forgetting we have an advantage. We can sway his thinking."

She gave Matt a worried look. "It didn't work with Lang."

"Unfortunately."

"Do we know why?"

"Maybe because his own nasty image of himself was so much a part of him that he wouldn't listen to anyone else."

"I hope that's true. And I hope it's not true of Harrison."

They negotiated through email for several hours and finally agreed to meet the detective early in the morning alone in the parking lot of a shopping center where they hoped they could make a quick getaway, if necessary.

MATT AND ELIZABETH said goodbye to the women they'd rescued and also Donna Martinson.

The women from The Mansion were still adjusting to their new freedom, but Donna took Elizabeth and Matt aside with a worried look on her face.

"Can you keep them out of any investigation?" she asked.

"That's what we're trying to do," Matt answered.

"But it might not be possible," she countered.

"I think it is," Matt said, praying that it was true. "In any case, we won't be coming back here."

They left Donna still looking worried.

In the car, Matt picked up on Elizabeth's troubled thoughts. "We can only do our best."

"Which better be good enough."

On the way to the shopping center, they discussed how they would handle the detective.

"The first question is—can we trust him?" Elizabeth asked.

"I think he's gotten a pretty good idea of what kind of people we are," Matt answered.

"Not telepaths."

He laughed. "No. Innocent victims caught in a mess they didn't make. And he's going to want to go to bat for us."

"We hope."

"We're going to reinforce that."

They stopped in an area where a few cars were parked and watched the place where they'd said they would meet.

Harrison kept his word and drove up alone in an unmarked car across from a fast-food restaurant.

Matt and Elizabeth made him wait for ten minutes before pulling up nose to tail with his vehicle.

The driver of each car rolled down his window so they could talk.

The detective began with "You know I don't usually do this kind of thing."

"We understand, and we appreciate it."

"Why the cloak-and-dagger stuff if you're innocent?"

"We told you Derek Lang was running a house of prostitution," Matt said.

"And bringing women illegally into the Port of Baltimore," the detective added.

Matt winced. He hadn't disclosed that information, but Harrison had figured it out. "We were hoping to leave out that part."

Elizabeth jumped into the conversation. "His death has stopped the traffic, and we don't want to involve any of the women, but we want to make sure we're not murder suspects. That's why we're meeting like this."

Leave the women out of it, Matt said, projecting the suggestion to the detective. *Leave the women out of it. They don't have to be involved. Lang's dead, and Delano and Forester were innocently involved.*

He repeated the silent words over and over, and they watched the man's face, both of them praying that he was going to come to the right conclusions.

"What exactly happened at Lang's bordello last night?" Harrison asked.

Chapter Sixteen

The tricky question, Matt thought.

"We went to rescue the women. Lang caught us there. He tied Elizabeth up and started torturing her. He had the guy named Southwell take me away to the basement."

"And how did you get away?"

"I was able to escape when the shooting started upstairs," Matt said. "Elizabeth was tied up when one of Lang's guards came in and shot him."

"Why?" Harrison asked.

"No idea," Matt answered.

We were there at the wrong time, Matt silently added. *We must have walked into a dispute between Lang and one of his men. We were lucky to escape with our lives.*

"I guess you were lucky to get out of there alive," Harrison said, and Matt breathed out a little sigh. The guy was buying it.

"The guard named Tony shot Lang. Southwell shot Tony."

"And how did you get away?"

"I untied Elizabeth, and we fled."

"How did the fire start?"

Matt shook his head. "No idea."

We were lucky to get out alive, Matt repeated. *You don't want to punish us for rescuing a bunch of women who were in a terrible situation through no fault of their own.*

Harrison looked at Elizabeth. "You had amnesia. How did you get your memory back?"

"Bits and pieces started coming back to me." She cleared her throat. "Dr. Delano helped me by using hypnosis. Finally I remembered enough to know about Lang."

"And why didn't you come to the police?"

"I'd seen Lang at a reception talking to a police official."

Harrison's eyes narrowed. "Which one?"

"I don't remember."

Harrison snorted. "Convenient."

You know we're good citizens. You want to help us, and Lang's death closes the case, Matt suggested.

"I think Lang's death closes the case," the detective said. "But I'd like an official statement from both of you about your involvement."

"At the station house?" Matt asked.

"Yes."

If we could just disappear, I'd go that route, Matt said to Elizabeth. *But it's kind of inconvenient not being able to get to our money.*

And having a criminal investigation hanging over us.

Still he wished to hell he could read the man's mind. This could be a trap, or it could be the key to getting them out of trouble, but they'd still have to dance around the part about the women.

They followed Harrison to the station house, agreeing on what they were going to say as they drove.

There was a bad moment when they went inside, and Harrison took them to separate rooms.

Matt saw the look of panic on Elizabeth's face.

Just tell him what we agreed on. And if we have any questions, we can confer.

Harrison asked them each to write an account of what had happened since Elizabeth had crashed her car into a lamppost. He wrote about treating her, having Polly take her home, and Lang's thugs coming after her.

And he silently checked in with her several times, seeing

that she was writing a similar account without using exactly the same words.

The part with the women was tricky, but Elizabeth pled client confidentiality, and Matt said she had given him only minimal information about them.

HARRISON CAME IN to read Matt's account and ask a few questions.

"So we're cleared of any involvement in Mrs. Kramer's murder?" he asked.

"Yes."

He let out the breath he'd been holding. "Thank you for taking care of this."

"I can't shake the feeling that I'm being manipulated," Harrison said.

Matt kept his features even. "We've just told you what happened to us."

"Uh-huh. Are the two of you planning to stay in the Baltimore area?"

Matt hesitated. He had been thinking about what they had to do next, but he didn't want to share that with the detective.

"I think we're going to try to decompress," he said. "But we haven't made any firm plans."

"And while you were with Elizabeth, the two of you hooked up."

"Yeah," Matt clipped out. *And I don't want to discuss it.*

To his relief, they were out of the police station a couple hours after they'd entered.

HAROLD GODDARD HAD checked his clipping service and his online sources four times day, looking for any item that might pertain to Matthew Delano and the woman named Jane Doe. He knew the doctor and his patient had disappeared after the woman who'd taken in "Jane" had been murdered.

He also scanned through the online version of the *Baltimore Sun*—where an interesting item caught his eye because it involved Dr. Delano. A crime boss named Derek Lang had been shot to death in a bordello he owned outside the city. One of his own men had turned on him, for unknown reasons. And another one had taken out the killer.

Interestingly he'd been using the same gun that had killed Polly Kramer, the nurse who had taken in Jane Doe. And there was another piece of information at the end of the story. The woman who had been known as Jane Doe was actually named Elizabeth Forester.

Harold went to his Solomon Clinic database and looked up the Forester woman. He wasn't surprised to find out she was on the same list as Matthew Delano—the list of babies born as a result of fertility treatments by Dr. Solomon.

As he read that piece of information, the hairs on the back of his neck prickled. He'd been putting together men and women from the clinic, and here were two of them who had found each other all by themselves.

What were the odds of that? What were the implications? What were they going to do next?

He started digging for more information and found out where each of them lived, although he was pretty sure that he wasn't going to find them in separate dwellings.

They'd be together.

From the article it wasn't clear exactly how they'd been involved with the crime boss, but it seemed they'd escaped from a dangerous situation.

What was their next move?

He didn't know these people, but he had a good guess about what they were going to do. Swift and Branson had gone to Houma to investigate their backgrounds. He'd bet his government pension that Delano and Forester would do the same. Did he have to kill them? Or could he head them off?

Perhaps his first move was to send someone to search her house and his apartment.

"I GUESS WE CAN get back to normal life," Elizabeth murmured, as they headed for the car.

"What's normal?"

"If you put it that way, I don't know. But we should start by telling Donna Martinson that she and the women are in the clear."

"Right."

They made the call, both of them happy to relieve the director's mind.

"What now?" Matt asked.

"I want to go back to my house and get some clothes. And now that I've got my memories back, I thought of something else. My baby book. Maybe it has some clues."

"I guess it's all right to go there."

"You're not sure."

"Old habits die hard."

They drove to her neighborhood and parked out front, then walked to the back.

"I know you wanted to look at some of the papers in the office, but I think we should skip that for now," Matt said as they approached the door.

She answered with a little nod. "But I should get a spare key, so that we can lock up when we leave."

She went to the office, opened the middle desk drawer and took out the key she kept on one side.

"At least they left it. You know, I'm going to have to do stuff like get a new driver's license."

"Yeah. Maybe they've got you in the computer, and you just have to call up, explain what happened and ask for a new one."

She grimaced. "First I'd have to prove who I am."

"You have a point."

She looked at the name tags she'd saved from conferences. "I guess they're not going to accept those. But that gives me an idea. If I stop by work, they'll know me at the office."

"And as your doctor, I can verify that you were the woman I treated for amnesia at Memorial Hospital."

"I hope all that's going to work."

"Let's get your clothes and get out of here."

"And that baby book."

They climbed the stairs, and Elizabeth took a suitcase from her bedroom closet. She opened drawers, taking out T-shirts and jeans. Then she took some clothing from the hangers in the closet, glad to have some of her own things.

"The baby book is in a box at the top of the closet—on the left," she told Matt. He reached up to the shelf and brought down the book. It had a padded exterior covered with faded pink silk. In gray letters it read My Little Girl.

He handed it to Elizabeth, and she held it carefully.

"I guess my mom was excited about having a baby."

Opening the cover, she flipped through the pages. In the front was her birth announcement and then congratulatory cards.

She could sense Matt's restlessness as she went through the contents.

"Bring it along. We'll look at it later. I want to get out of here while the getting's good."

The words were just out of his mouth when they heard a door open and footsteps on the first floor.

They both froze, and she gave him a panicked look.

Did you lock the door behind us? Matt asked.

Yes. Do you think it could be one of Lang's men down there?

I'm betting they got out of town—the ones who could still travel.

So who is that?

I'd like to know. But we've got one thing going for us. He's taking his time. He must not know we're here.

They listened as whoever it was pawed through kitchen drawers, then ambled down the hall to the office. After he rummaged around in there for a while, he headed for the stairs.

It sounds like only one intruder.

Unless he's got a lookout down there. Get behind the door.

Elizabeth flattened herself against the wall, waiting tensely as she read what Matt had in mind.

The man apparently didn't know his way around the house. When he reached the second floor, he walked into the guest room, stayed for a few minutes, then headed for Elizabeth's bedroom.

As he walked through the door, Matt hit him with a bolt of power. He staggered back, but he stayed on his feet and pulled out a gun.

Chapter Seventeen

Elizabeth was in back of the intruder.

"Over here," she called out.

When he whirled, Matt hit him with another bolt, and Elizabeth added her strength.

This time the man went down.

Matt leaped on him, stepping on his gun hand, making the intruder scream. And Elizabeth picked up the lamp on the bedside table and brought it down on his head. He went still.

"What do you have that we can use to tie him up?"

"What about duct tape—like we used before?"

"Yeah."

She hurried down the hall to the guest room and came back with a roll of tape, and Matt used it to secure the man.

He groaned and blinked.

"Whaa…?" he asked.

"What are you doing here?"

When he pressed his lips together. Matt kicked him in the ribs, and he let out a yelp.

"You'd better tell us what's going on, if you don't want worse."

Elizabeth made a silent suggestion. *Maybe we can use the persuasion technique on him.*

Matt focused on the man. *You don't want me to hurt you again. You want to tell us what's going on. You want to tell us who sent you.*

The man looked confused as Matt continued to project the message.

"Who sent you?" Elizabeth asked.

"I don't know."

"What do you mean, you don't know? How did you end up in this house?"

"A contact told me the job came from New Orleans. That's all I know."

New Orleans! Matt echoed. *What about New Orleans?* he silently pressed.

"What about New Orleans?" Elizabeth echoed the question.

"Someone down there wants the scoop on you. That's all I know. I swear."

Matt gave him another treatment, but he didn't come up with any more information.

I think that's all he's got.

She nodded.

"How were you going to get paid?"

"I was supposed to leave a message at a phone number. Then I'd get the money from PayPal."

Matt snorted. "Criminals are using PayPal?"

The man shrugged.

They left him on the floor and stepped out of the room.

"Hey," he yelled, "you can't just leave me here."

"Watch us."

Elizabeth put the baby book in the suitcase along with the clothing, and they hurried downstairs.

"Better leave the door unlocked so the cops can get in," he said.

When they were outside, Matt pulled out his cell phone and dialed Detective Harrison. The call went straight to voice mail, which was a relief to Matt.

He left a message saying, "We went to Elizabeth Forester's house to get some of her clothing, and we were surprised by an intruder. We restrained him, and you can find him in the master bedroom."

"Is that legal?" Elizabeth asked.

"I hope so. But I'm not going to wait around."

"What if he says he was there for a legitimate reason?"

"Like what? You called him to fix the water heater?"

"I guess not."

"I'm hoping his fingerprints are in the criminal database. I'll check later with Harrison on that."

She sighed. "The cops are going to be all over the house."

"Do you care?"

"I guess not. After Lang's men came through, I don't think I can live there again."

He put his arm around her and pulled her close. "When this is over, we'll decide where to live."

She nodded against his shoulder, then caught what was in his mind. "We're going to New Orleans?"

"I was thinking we might poke into that fertility clinic. Now with this guy showing up, I think we have to."

"Yes."

She could see he was turning over possibilities. "You don't want to fly."

"I don't want our names on a passenger list that someone could check. Which means we should drive."

"All right. Then let's not push ourselves."

She knew he was anxious to get there, but he said, "Yeah, we can stop along the way to practice our skills. And do some research."

Elizabeth checked in with Social Services and told them she wasn't ready to return to work. It turned out she had months of sick leave she could use. And Dr. Delano was happy to say she still needed to rest. She also got a new driver's license, and Matt checked in with Detective Harrison. When they found out the guy who'd burglarized Elizabeth's house was a known criminal named Walter Clemens, they went down to make a complaint.

"You two seem to attract trouble," the detective said.

"We're hoping to change that," Matt answered.

"How?"

"We're going on a road trip."

"How will that help?"

"It will get us out of town."

Matt checked back in at Memorial Hospital and took a leave of absence.

"What if they won't take you back?" Elizabeth asked.

"There's always a need for doctors. I'll be able to get a job somewhere."

After they'd made their arrangements, they mapped out a route to New Orleans.

"It looks like about an eighteen-hour trip," Matt said. "We could shoot for six to eight hours of driving a day."

Their first stop was Roanoke, which had initially been called Big Lick because of the nearby salt lick that attracted wildlife. The town had been a major stop for wagon trains going west. Coal and the manufacturer of steam engines had made the city prosperous.

"Too bad we aren't here for the Big Lick Blues Festival or the Strawberry Festival," Elizabeth said as she looked up information about the city.

"I think we can have our own festival," Matt answered as he drove past several chain motels.

She grinned at him, letting the images in his brain warm her, still thinking how lucky she was to have found this man.

"The feeling's mutual," he said as he pulled into the parking lot of an upscale motel.

"How LONG WERE you going to keep the information from me?" Jake Harper asked his wife.

Rachel looked up from the table in her New Orleans shop

where she read tarot cards. They were in the city—where they spent about half their time, when they weren't at the plantation in Lafayette that Gabriella Boudreaux had established as a refuge for telepaths. Rachel raised her face toward her husband. "I guess I wasn't going to keep it from you for very long."

"Do you know who they are?"

"Her name is Elizabeth. His is Matt."

"You found them when they were on the East Coast. Are they still there? Or are they doing what other bonded couples have done—looking for their origins?"

She sighed. "I think they're on the way to Houma."

"And are they a threat to us? Like Tanya and Mickey." The first couple they'd encountered like themselves.

"I think Tanya and Mickey were unusual," Rachel said. "They didn't want anyone to share their powers."

"But you don't know for sure, because you always want to see the best in people."

"I can't help what I am."

Jake walked up beside his wife's chair and slung his arm around her shoulder. "I love what you are."

She leaned back against him, reassured by what they were together. She was impulsive. He was cautious, which was often a good thing for both of them.

"Is the same man after them who was after Stephanie and Craig?" he asked, happy they could protect the newcomers who had recently come to the plantation.

"They ran into some bad problems in Baltimore—that didn't have anything to do with the Solomon Clinic."

She opened her mind fully to her husband and let him see some of what had happened to Elizabeth and Matt.

He winced. "It sounds like they're lucky to be alive."

"Because they're resourceful. They'd be a big asset to our community. Especially since he's a doctor."

"An asset, yeah," Jake agreed. "If they don't want to wipe us off the face of the earth. Are they flying down here?"

"They're driving."

"That should give us time to prepare."

"For the worst?"

"You know I have to think of worst-case scenarios."

"But we know some important things about them. He risked his life treating patients in Africa. She was going up against a man smuggling women into Baltimore and forcing them into prostitution. That means neither one of them is selfish—like Mickey and Tanya."

Jake nodded. "Those are good signs."

In their motel room, after making wonderful love with Matt, Elizabeth finally turned to the baby book she'd brought from Baltimore.

There were records of when she'd first eaten solid food, when she'd taken her first steps, and her first words—which were "dog" and "doll."

"My mother was pretty compulsive about writing things down," Elizabeth commented.

She turned a page, and her hand froze. There was a picture of her standing in front of a building. The sign beside the door read Solomon Clinic.

Matt stared at the picture. "I guess that must be the place. But what were you doing there? I mean, you look like you were maybe three."

"Yes. And I don't know why I went back there."

"But we do know it's in Houma."

Clemens, the man who'd gone snooping in Elizabeth Forester's house, had gotten into bad trouble. He was in jail, and Harold Goddard didn't like it, but now he had no choice.

He was certain that Forester and Delano were on their way to Houma. He had checked passenger lists on flights from Baltimore and found nothing. That wasn't reassuring. It just meant that the couple was being tricky. Probably they were driving, so no one could track their arrival.

Harold had been thinking about how to protect himself. Now he put that plan into action.

ELIZABETH FELT THEY were finally getting somewhere, when she went to sleep. She woke with a start in the middle of the night, her whole body rigid.

Matt was instantly awake beside her. Rolling toward her, he took her in his arms. "What is it?"

"Someone touched my mind."

"What does that mean?"

"I mean, it's like when you and I communicate without talking. Only it wasn't you." She clenched her fist in frustration. "Well, it wasn't exactly someone communicating with me. They were…probing."

He sucked in a sharp breath. "You're sure?"

"I didn't make it up. I felt another mind…skimming mine."

"You were asleep. You could have dreamed."

"I don't think so. But that could be true."

When she started to tremble, he pulled her closer.

"Something else we need to worry about," she whispered.

"Was it a man or a woman?"

"I'm not sure. If I had to guess, I'd say it was a woman."

"Why?"

She laughed. "Because she was delicate…subtle."

"You don't think men can be subtle?"

"It's not the way they normally operate."

He stroked her arm. "I guess you're right.

Is this woman a threat to us?" He reached for her hand and knitted his fingers with hers, and she tightened her grip.

"I wish I knew."

"We talked about practicing our skills on this trip. I think shielding our minds should be one of our top priorities."

She nodded against his shoulder. She'd thought they were safe—at least for a little while. Now she was a lot less sure. And she knew she wasn't going back to sleep any time soon.

Matt packed up on the observation. "We can start practicing now."

"Because you know I'm worried?" she asked, although she already knew the answer.

"Because it's the right thing to do."

He sat up, and she did the same, pulling up the pillow and leaning against the headboard.

When he climbed out of bed, she gave him a questioning look.

Better if we're not touching.

You mean, easier.

He pulled on a T-shirt and his shorts, and sat down in the chair near the window.

I'm going to block my thoughts. You try to worm your way in.

A nice way to put it. How do you block your thoughts?

I don't know exactly. I guess we'll find out.

Chapter Eighteen

"I'm going to picture a wall and put it up around my mind," Matt suggested.

"Will that work?"

"I hope it's better than picturing a mud hole."

She laughed. "I guess so." She gave him a long look. "Okay, you put up your wall, then think of something you want to guard behind it."

She could sense the barrier going into place. She could even see it in his mind. It was made of cement blocks, and he put it together block by block.

Then she knew by his expression that he'd hidden a thought behind it.

She had very little trouble breaking through. And when she did, she laughed.

"You're thinking about the food we're going to get in New Orleans," she said.

"Yeah."

"Try again."

He gritted his teeth and went back to the wall, and this time she had a little more trouble breaking through. When she did, she gave him a long look. "You've switched from food to sex."

"I'm a guy, after all. Maybe I put them in the wrong order. Why don't we reverse the process, and you try?"

She focused her gaze inward, constructing a barrier out of sturdy upright metal pieces. When she had it in place, she put an image of a beautiful garden inside, then put herself in the picture, sitting down in a wicker chair, enjoying the sunlight slanting through the trees.

It was hard to keep the wall in place and keep the image of the garden at the same time, but she managed it for a few minutes until Matt came along and started pulling her stakes out of the ground.

"No fair," she said aloud.

"Everything's fair."

"Oh, is it?" She heated up the metal stakes, making them too hot for him to handle.

"Nice move," he said.

"We're just playing around."

"But everything we do is practice for when we need to use it."

RACHEL HAD ANOTHER report for Jake in the morning. "She felt me probing her, and she's trying to shield her mind."

He cursed under his breath. "That means they have something to hide."

"Don't jump to conclusions."

"Then what?"

"Suppose you'd felt an outside presence trying to read your thoughts, wouldn't you try to keep him from doing it?"

"That's one explanation."

"But you think they have evil intentions?"

"I want to keep you safe."

"You're always so suspicious."

"I guess it comes from my early childhood experiences."

She reached for his hand. Jake had grown up on the streets of New Orleans, and he'd learned never to trust anyone until he'd proved himself.

"Did you get into his mind?" he asked.

"She's more open."

"Why?"

"Like I said, he was a doctor in Africa. I think he learned caution on a lot of different levels."

"And they're on their way down here?"

"Yes."

"I guess we'd better be prepared."

"How?"

"Keep trying to figure out what they're up to."

"On the other hand, maybe it's better if I don't try to dip into her mind."

ELIZABETH AND MATT left the motel after breakfast and got back on the road, keeping up their practice sessions as they drove.

But there were some things Elizabeth couldn't hide from Matt. The closer they got to New Orleans, the more unsettled she felt, and he picked up on her mood.

"You think we're going to be in danger when we get there," he said, not bothering to frame the statement as a question. "From whoever that Clemens guy is working for."

"Unfortunately." She turned her head toward him. "When is it going to stop?"

"Soon."

"How do you know?"

"Because I think there's got to be a quick resolution. Like we came to with Lang."

"That's not exactly reassuring." She reached to cover his hand with her own. "I got you into a lot of trouble."

"You know damn well we're in this together."

She understood that as much as she'd understood anything in her life and pressed her palm more firmly against the back of his hand. "I wouldn't have gotten my memory back or gotten away from Lang without you, but now I'm wondering if we're making a mistake."

He waited for her to say more, although he probably knew what was in her mind.

"I think we should do some research before we get down there. You can use the web to look up that fertility clinic."

"Agreed."

WHEN THEY STOPPED for the night in Huntsville, Alabama, they had an early dinner at a ribs restaurant. Then they returned to their motel room, and Matt used his computer to get on the web.

Because the Solomon Clinic had been closed for twenty years, there wasn't much information about the facility. But it had been run by a Dr. Douglas Solomon, and there was a piece of startling information about him.

"According to a newspaper article, he had a research facility in Houma that blew up a few months ago."

"Did he die?"

"Yeah. He was inside at the time. Also one of the nurses that used to work at the fertility clinic died with him. And another man who apparently used to run a government think tank."

"What was he doing there?"

"No idea."

Elizabeth winced. "Do they know what caused the explosion?"

"The article says it was a gas leak, but I find it pretty jarring that just before we started poking into Dr. Solomon's background, he got killed."

"You're saying you don't think it was an accident?"

"I don't know what to think, except that we should be even more cautious."

She shuddered, wanting to say that they should just turn around and go back to Baltimore.

"Only we'll always be looking over our shoulder, waiting for something else to happen," he said.

She answered with a little nod, knowing he was right.

"First we'll go to New Orleans and poke around," she said, thinking that she was only postponing the day of reckoning.

"No. I think we're going to find something there," he said.

"Not the guy who hired Clemens, I hope."

"He won't know we're in the city."

"Unless he has some way of finding out who's checked into hotels."

"That would take a lot of digging."

They arrived in New Orleans the next day and found a charming bed-and-breakfast in the French Quarter, a place where Elizabeth would have loved to stay if they'd been here on vacation. But she was too restless to enjoy their antique-filled suite or the old-fashioned claw-foot tub in the bathroom.

Matt looked at her with concern. "Maybe we shouldn't have come."

"You know we have to. And I want to walk around a little bit and get a feel for the city."

They headed for Jackson Square, where they watched the street performers and wandered around the stands where artists were offering to do quick sketches of tourists, and women had set up card tables where they were selling tarot cards and palm readings.

"Do you remember it?" Matt asked.

"Yes. I guess it hasn't changed much in twenty-five years. But I want to see something else."

"Something you remember?"

"No." Elizabeth walked rapidly along one side of the square, then took a side street leading to Toulouse Street.

"If you haven't been here before, you seem to know where you're going," Matt commented.

She shrugged. "Not really."

"You're just…wandering?"

She knew he didn't think that was true. Perhaps she didn't, either. She scanned the shops along Toulouse and stopped at an inviting little storefront that offered tarot-card readings by a woman named Rachel Harper.

"You walked past the readers in the square," Matt said. "Why are you stopping here?"

"This woman interests me."

"Why? Do you know her?"

"No."

"Then what is it about her? Is she more insightful because she has her own shop?"

"She made enough money to buy it."

"Or maybe a rich husband set her up."

Elizabeth snorted and peered at the Closed sign in the door. "I wonder when she's coming back."

"We can try again later," Matt said. "If you think it's important."

"It could be. I don't know," she said uncertainly. "Or maybe it's nothing." She dragged in a breath and let it out. "It's weird. When I first met you, I didn't remember anything. Now I do, and I'm also…" She flung her arm. "I don't know what to call it. Having insights?"

"Maybe part of your mental abilities." He examined the door and window of the shop. "You'd think she'd let customers know how to get in touch with her. But there doesn't seem to be anybody here."

They kept walking through the French Quarter, both of them on edge, but still able to enjoy the colorful buildings, art galleries, antique shops and tropical flowers that were so different from Baltimore.

When Elizabeth stopped in front of a restaurant, Matt gave her an inquiring look.

"You want to eat here?" he asked.

"Not necessarily. But I'm getting the same kind of feeling I did from Rachel Harper's shop."

She stood on the sidewalk for a minute, then walked on.

"Or maybe I'm making stuff up because I want to have something significant happen."

"Maybe it's not going to happen in the city."

At breakfast the next morning, as they enjoyed beignets, strong Louisiana coffee and omelets with andouille sausage, Elizabeth said, "I'd like to go back and see if Rachel Harper is there."

"Not by yourself. Not until we find out about that clinic."

She nodded, knowing he was right. They were safer if they stuck together. But safer from what? She still didn't know.

They both walked back to Rachel Harper's shop, but the tarot-card reader still wasn't there.

A woman across the street stuck her head out of a doorway and asked, "Are you looking for Ms. Harper?"

"Yes."

"She's only here part-time—since she got married."

"Thanks," Elizabeth answered, feeling let down. Turning to Matt, she said, "We should go to Houma and see what we can find out about the clinic."

"I did some more research after you went to sleep last night," he said.

"And?"

"I told you that a nurse who had worked there died in the explosion with Dr. Solomon."

"But what?" She cut him a quick look. "You're keeping me from knowing what you're thinking."

"Good because the technique is working. There's another one of Solomon's staffers living at a nursing home in Houma. Her name's Maven Bolton. Maybe there's something she can tell us about Dr. Solomon's operation."

"Did you look up Houma?" Elizabeth asked.

"Yes. The population is around 33,000. You can book swamp tours and fishing expeditions, eat spicy Cajun food and walk bird trails in the wildlife park."

"The town's not all that large. I mean for someone to locate an important clinic there."

"Maybe he wanted a specific kind of environment. It has a long and proud past, and a historic downtown area. The Terrebonne Parish Courthouse is there, which would mean it was a center of local activity."

"Was there anything about the Solomon Clinic?"

"Actually I know where it used to be."

"I'd like to see it. How far away is it?"

"A little over an hour."

"We can have lunch in town."

They arrived on schedule and drove around Houma, noting that the historic center was probably much as it had been for years, with newer development on the outskirts.

As they crossed a bridge, Elizabeth said, "The place is full of rivers and bayous."

"Yes. It's almost like some of the sections of town are islands."

"It's got a lot of atmosphere, but just being here makes me feel…nervous," Elizabeth mused as they drove up and down tree-shaded streets where large old houses sat on generous plots. She was silent for several moments, then said, "Can you find Dr. Solomon's lab? The one where he was killed?"

Matt consulted his smartphone, where he'd put some addresses. "It's not too far from here."

He punched the street and number into the GPS, and they drove for a few more blocks, stopping in front of a large red-brick house that had been heavily damaged. Behind it was another building that was totally destroyed.

"Why did he have his lab in a residential area?" Elizabeth asked. "Did he live here, too?"

"Actually this was the home of the nurse who died."

"Which implied that they had some sort of close relationship. I want to get out," Elizabeth whispered. Even when she knew Matt thought it was a bad idea, she opened the door and exited the car.

Behind her, he pulled closer to the curb, cut the engine and followed her up the driveway. She stood for a moment, staring at the house with its boarded-up windows and blackened bricks, then skirted around to the real scene of destruction.

She could see an enormous hole in the ground, filled with debris. Pieces of wood, cinder blocks, medical equipment and furniture were scattered around the rubble.

"It looks like nobody's been here to clean up," she whispered as Matt came up behind her.

"Maybe there's a question of ownership."

She looked up and down the street at the well-kept houses and yards.

"They can't leave it forever," he said, following her thoughts.

She made a derisive sound. "There was a swimming pool in Baltimore that kids used all the time. I mean kids whose parents couldn't afford a country club. The owner tore it down, and we all thought they had sold the land for houses or apartments. That was fifteen years ago, and it's still sitting empty."

"But the pool owners didn't leave a mess, did they?"

"No."

Matt nodded and stepped closer to the pit, looking down into the tangle of debris.

"I see a lot of medical equipment—some of it expensive."

"Like what?"

He pointed. "There's a mangled X-ray machine. A couple exam tables. Cabinets that probably held drugs. An EKG machine. Centrifuges. A spectrophotometer. It looks like the doctor had plenty of money to spend on his research project."

"I wonder what he was doing. Do you think it was related to the clinic?"

"Or something new. It looks like it was paying off." He turned to her. "We shouldn't stick around here."

"I know. I just wanted to see what it looked like." She shuddered. "And try to figure out what happened. You think this place was really destroyed by a gas leak?"

"I don't know." He dragged in a breath and let it out. "I don't smell anything like explosives."

"It was a few months ago."

He picked up a stick from the ground, walked to a pile of debris and turned over some charred pieces of wood and paper.

"But the smell would linger," he said.

"What else could do so much damage?"

"I'd like to know."

She gave him a long look. "If…uh…somebody had a lot of time to practice, do you think they could blow up a building the way we've been zapping people and rocks?"

His head whipped toward her. "You're thinking people like us could have done it?"

"Could they?"

"Not just two people, I don't think."

She shivered. "What if…"

He waited for her to finish the thought, but she shrugged. "I'm not going there."

They returned to the car and Matt pulled away, checking in his rearview mirror as he turned the corner.

"You think someone could follow us from here?" Elizabeth asked.

"It could be under surveillance, and I'm not taking any chances."

He kept checking behind them as they headed for the business district where they found several restaurants and some antique shops.

"There's where the clinic used to be," Matt said, pointing to a building that looked more modern than many of those around it.

"Was it torn down?"

"I don't know."

"Maybe Mrs. Bolton can enlighten us. I guess it's time to talk to her." Elizabeth sighed. "I wonder why I want to put it off."

"Maybe you're afraid you're not going to like what we hear."

"Then let's get it over with and eat later. The more we know, the better off we are."

They arrived at the nursing home before lunch. The facility was an attractive looking one-story redbrick residence and nursing facility for the elderly.

"I hope we can get something out of this interview," Elizabeth said as they pulled into the parking lot and Matt cut the engine. "I mean, if she's in a nursing home, maybe her mind is going."

"Or maybe she's just not capable of living on her own."

Elizabeth nodded, trying not to dwell on her doubts as she scanned the building and grounds. "It's well maintained."

"It might be a nice place to retire," Matt said as they followed a winding path through well-tended gardens.

Just beyond the double doors was a reception area where a young woman sat at an antique desk.

Her name tag identified her as Sarah Dalton.

"Can I help you?" she asked in a gracious southern accent.

"We'd like to visit with Maven Bolton."

She tipped her head to one side, studying them. "Another couple to visit Maven. I wonder why she's gotten very popular."

"There have been other couples coming to see her?" Matt asked.

"Why, yes. Two others."

"Who?"

"I didn't know them. But Maven told me that one of the women was named Rachel."

Elizabeth tensed. "From New Orleans?"

"I don't know for sure. How do you know Maven?"

"We…we're old friends," Matt answered.

"They were, as well."

That sounds weird. Should we leave? Elizabeth silently asked Matt.

No.

But who were they? I mean, could Rachel have been the tarot-card reader?

Maybe we'll find out.

"I'm sure she'll be pleased to see you," Ms. Dalton said. "Maven should be in the dayroom now."

They followed the employee down a wide hallway with nature pictures on the walls, to a pleasantly large recreation room with windows looking out onto the gardens.

About twenty women and a few men were sitting around the room. Some were in wheelchairs. Others were in easy chairs watching television or at tables playing cards or working puzzles.

Ms. Dalton led them to a woman who was seated by the window with a magazine in her lap. She had short gray hair and a wrinkled face, and she was wearing a nice-looking black-and-white blouse and black slacks.

"Some people to see you, Maven."

The older woman looked up a bit apprehensively.

"We just stopped in to say hello," Matt said. They both pulled up chairs and sat down.

After a few moments the attendant left them.

The old woman silently studied the visitors. "Are you like that other couple?"

The receptionist had also said something similar.

"I don't know. What can you tell us about them?" Elizabeth said carefully, pulling her chair a little closer.

"They were both getting married. They wanted information about…the Solomon Clinic."

Elizabeth tried to keep her voice even and her face neutral while her heart was clunking inside her chest so hard that she was surprised her blouse wasn't moving up and down. "Why?"

"I shouldn't talk about it. It was supposed to be a secret."

Chapter Nineteen

Elizabeth looked at Matt, then back at the old woman who might be able to tell them what had really been going on at the Solomon Clinic.

But you want to tell us about the clinic. You worked there years ago. It's all right to talk about it now.

Maven looked uncertain, and Matt repeated the suggestion and added, *It's all right to talk to us. We won't tell anyone else.*

Elizabeth waited with her heart pounding for the woman to speak.

Maven lowered her voice. "Their mothers had fertility treatments from Dr. Solomon."

"That's not so unusual," Matt answered.

"Yes. But Dr. Solomon doesn't like me to talk about that. Not since the clinic burned down."

"It burned?"

"Why, yes. It was at night, so nobody was hurt, thank the Lord."

I guess she doesn't know Solomon's dead, Matt silently commented.

And from her tone of voice, it seems she was afraid of him.

"We won't tell anyone," Elizabeth repeated Matt's earlier assurance. She gently put her hand on the old woman's arm. "What can you tell us?"

Matt soundlessly reinforced the question.

"Well, you know, the doctor ran it like a fertility clinic.

That's how he got the babies. But he was really doing experiments on those children before they were born. He thought we didn't know, well, all except Dorothy. She was his pet."

"Experiments?" Elizabeth asked carefully. "What was he trying to do to them?"

"Make them supersmart," the old woman said as though she were confiding the nuclear-launch codes. "That's why he had the children come back for tests. But he was disappointed because they didn't seem any different from ordinary children."

"He was doing brain experiments?" Matt asked.

"Didn't I say that?"

"Not exactly."

"He was so excited when he started. He was sure his techniques were going to produce something extraordinary. Then he couldn't understand why they weren't working." The woman's expression suddenly closed. "I shouldn't be talking to you about any of this." She raised her head. "I should call Sarah."

"No need," Matt said. "We won't ask you any more questions."

She turned her head away, and Elizabeth looked up to see that some of the residents were staring at the scene.

We're attracting attention.

We'd better go.

She and Matt got up and left the dayroom, then hurried down the hall, retracing their steps.

"I think we found out what we wanted to know about the clinic," Matt said when they were back in the hall. "I think he was working with fertilized eggs, operating on the blastocytes, the first hundred cells that develop."

"Back then? Isn't that kind of advanced?"

"I guess you could say he was a genius."

"An evil genius. He was using eggs he had no right to. He was playing with people's lives."

"Obviously he thought the end justified the means. And he didn't care who got hurt in the process. But it didn't work out the way he thought it would. He was altering these babies' brains, but instead of making them smart, he created potential telepaths."

She nodded.

"And creating people who were doomed to lead miserable lives—unless they met someone else who was a product of the experiment."

"How many more of us are there, do you think?" Elizabeth asked.

"That's something we should try to find out."

"And it sounds like we're not the first couple that got together."

They both stopped short as they considered the implications.

"Let's say that the woman who was probing my thoughts is one of us," she said.

"That's a stretch."

"Who else?"

He shrugged.

"And let's say that, for some reason, she and her partner blew up Dr. Solomon's clinic."

"An even bigger stretch," Matt said. "But an important question is, are the other people friendly to each other or hostile?"

She sucked in a sharp breath. "Why would they be hostile?"

"I don't know. I'm trying to consider every angle."

"Like what?"

"Okay, then, who is it that was trying to get information about us—at your house? Some of the other adults who were born as a result of the project?"

"Or someone else."

They had reached the front door, and Matt pulled it open.

She grabbed his arm, stopping him from walking out on the porch.

"What?" Matt asked.

"There's a car next to ours."

"Another visitor."

"I don't think so."

As they watched, two men got out. Both of them were wearing sport shirts, casual slacks and what looked like football helmets.

Matt stared at them. *Football helmets?*

I don't like it.

When they saw Elizabeth and Matt they started rapidly up the walk toward the building, and the expressions on their faces weren't particularly friendly.

"What are we going to do now?" she asked.

"Find the back exit."

The receptionist looked up at them as they hurried down the hall in the direction they'd just come from.

"You can't just go back there again," she called.

Matt turned toward her.

Two men are headed this way. They're thugs. Keep them from following us.

Praying that the mental suggestion was going to give them a little extra time, Elizabeth kept pace with Matt.

He took a side hallway, then dodged into one of the rooms. A woman was in a hospital bed watching television. She looked up in alarm as two strangers charged into her room.

"Who are you?"

We're friends. Just keep calm. Don't tell anyone we were here, Matt instructed as he crossed to the window.

It was of the casement variety, and he turned the crank, then used his foot to knock out the screen.

"Go on," he said to Elizabeth.

With no other choice, she swung one leg over the sill,

then levered herself the rest of the way out, glad that it was only a few feet to the ground.

Come on, she called to Matt.

I wish I could close the window, but I can't crank it from the outside.

Just get out of there.

To her relief, Matt stuck his foot out the window, then his head and shoulder. He lowered himself to the lawn, and they looked around. The grounds of the nursing home were well kept, but beyond them was a scraggly area that bordered one of the bayous that cut across the town.

Can we make it to the car? Elizabeth asked.

Not directly. He looked toward the scruffy area, where the trees and bushes would give them some cover. *Maybe we can work our way around.*

You think there are just the two guys?

I wish I knew.

Why are they after us? Elizabeth asked.

I'm guessing someone has a clue about the children from the Solomon Clinic, and they want more information. Or they are children from the clinic, and they know we could screw with their minds—so they rigged up some protective gear.

Unfortunately.

From inside the nursing home, they could hear running feet and knew they didn't have much time to make a getaway.

Matt took the lead, moving alongside the building until they were closer to the wooded area.

When the distance was as short as it was going to get, he looked back at Elizabeth. *I'm going first. If I make it across without getting shot, you follow.*

His thoughts confirmed that he hated putting it that way, but he didn't see any alternative.

With her heart in her mouth, she watched Matt dash across the open space to the scrubby patch of land beyond the manicured lawn.

When he raised his hand and waved at her, she breathed out a little sigh of relief. In the next second, she saw his expression change to one of horror.

Before she could figure out what was wrong, a hand closed over her shoulder.

"Move and I'll shoot you in the kneecap," a harsh voice said.

RACHEL HARPER STOOD frozen in the living room of her cottage at the Lafayette plantation. When the door burst open, she whirled as Stephanie Swift charged through the door. Craig Branson was right behind her. They were both products of Dr. Solomon's illegal experiments.

A few months earlier, Stephanie had been trapped into an engagement to a man named John Reynard, a criminal who'd insinuated himself into New Orleans society. Then she'd met Craig Branson and had known she was about to make a horrible mistake by going through with that marriage.

When Reynard had whisked Stephanie away to his heavily fortified plantation, Craig had followed.

Rachel and Jake had helped them escape from Reynard's men—and also from thugs sent by someone else. And now they were all at the plantation owned by Gabriella Boudreaux, who was paired with Luke Buckley.

"It's the same man who was after me and Craig," Stephanie gasped as they rushed into Rachel's cottage.

"You saw what just happened?"

"Yes." She flushed. "I mean, I knew you were upset. You were broadcasting it like a television cop show."

They were followed very quickly by Gabriella and Luke.

Rachel turned as her husband, Jake Harper, came into the room.

"What's happening, exactly?" he asked.

"I wasn't sure what was going on until now," Rachel

breathed. "That other couple—Elizabeth and Matt—are from Baltimore. It's a long story, but they found a man burglarizing Elizabeth's house and got from him that he was hired by someone in New Orleans. They'd already started doing research on the Solomon Clinic and went to Houma. They found the same nursing home we did and talked to Maven. But thugs were waiting for them when they came out."

"They just grabbed Elizabeth," Stephanie added. "And they're wearing some kind of protective helmets."

"Helmets?" Jake asked. "Why?"

"Because they know we have mental powers, and the helmets must have some kind of lining that blocks us," Stephanie said.

Jake swore under his breath.

"We have to go there," Stephanie said. "We have to help them."

The men looked doubtful.

Rachel swung toward the other women, exchanging silent messages before focusing on Jake. "You guys may not be coming, but we have to go to Houma."

"If you think we're letting the three of you go there alone, you're crazy," Jake said.

"Is that a sexist opinion?" she asked.

"It's the opinion of a man who loves his wife and doesn't want to send her into danger."

"But we have to go," Stephanie answered.

Jake apparently knew when he was outvoted. "We'll take the van. And we'll make plans on the way. It's almost a two-hour drive."

"Will we be in time?" Stephanie asked.

"We can only pray we will be," Rachel answered.

Rachel's gaze turned inward as she tuned in on the scene in Houma.

Jake heard her gasp. *What?*

Maybe it's already too late, she said.

MATT STARED IN HORROR as one of the helmeted men reached for Elizabeth and pulled her against his body in a parody of an embrace.

"We've got your girlfriend," he called out. "If you don't want to see her get shot, you'd better come back here."

Stay away. Don't do it, he heard Elizabeth shouting in his mind. But how could he leave her with the men?

We'll think of something.

But what? He tried sending a mental suggestion to the man who held Elizabeth. *Let her go. You don't want to hold her. Let her go.* But the silent order had no effect.

Matt wanted to spit out a string of curses, but that wasn't going to do him any good. He understood the problem. The man knew what he and Elizabeth could do, and he was wearing that football helmet thing to block any messages Matt and Elizabeth might try to send him.

But the two of them could still communicate with each other. And although they knew a mental command wasn't going to make her captor turn her loose, there might be another way.

"Why do you want us?" he called out.

"It's just a job for me."

"Then let us go."

"No way. Turn yourself in if you don't want something bad to happen to her."

I'm going to look like I'm giving up, he said to Elizabeth. *When I get about ten feet from you, act like you're going to faint.*

Okay.

Matt's gaze flicked to the left and right. At any moment, the other thug could show up, and that would create a problem he might not be able to overcome.

His heart was pounding so hard that he could barely breathe as he started back the way he'd come.

Chapter Twenty

Matt saw the tension on Elizabeth's face. He imagined that his own expression was just as grim.

As he walked, he gathered his energy, and he felt Elizabeth preparing to aid him. He might not be able to reach the man's mind, but that wasn't his only option.

He was about twenty feet from her captor when he silently shouted, *Now*.

Elizabeth went limp, as if the frightening situation had made her legs give out. The man scrambled to get control of her, but part of his attention had to stay on Matt. With only a small window of opportunity before the guy was in contact with her again, Matt shot out a jolt of energy, hitting him in the shoulder.

He yelped and reared back.

Elizabeth regained her footing immediately and dodged to the side, giving Matt another shot at the man.

The guy bellowed and went down. Elizabeth kicked him in the face, marveling at her new attitude toward violence. When he stilled, she bent to get the gun and took it out of his hands.

Do we keep this? she asked as she drew up beside Matt. He wanted to reach for her, but there was no time for anything but escape.

I'll take it.

He clicked the safety on and tucked the weapon into the waistband of his slacks.

The two of them ran for the scraggly underbrush, disappearing into the trees. But a shout followed them, and Matt knew that the other man had seen where they went.

No, not just one man. There were two others now.

One stopped by their fallen comrade. The other stayed behind Matt and Elizabeth.

STEPHANIE TURNED TO Rachel. "Are you following what's happening?"

"Yes. They got away from the bad guys, but armed men are chasing them alongside the bayou."

Frustration bubbled inside Stephanie. She'd been in a similar situation not so long ago.

Craig put a hand on her arm, trying to calm her.

"Is there anything we can do?" she asked.

"We can try." Rachel closed her eyes, her face a study in concentration as the two other women reached out to touch her. Stephanie felt Rachel trying to direct a surge of power toward the pursuers to at least slow them down, but at this distance, the task was impossible.

"We have to get closer." Rachel said.

She looked toward Jake, but everybody in the van already knew he was driving at a dangerous speed.

"We can't fly. And we aren't going to be any use to them if we crash," he muttered.

MATT AND ELIZABETH plunged farther into the wilderness area, dodging around cypress, tupelo trees and saw palmettos. They splashed through areas of standing water, mud clinging to their shoes and making it almost impossible to run.

Both of them were breathing hard, and he wondered how long they could sustain the pace. But they had to keep going because behind them he could hear the men getting closer, making no attempt to hide their progress through the underbrush.

Elizabeth looked back in panic, then pointed to their right. *If we go farther into the swamp, maybe they won't follow.*

We can try.

Matt veered off in the direction she'd suggested, and they worked their way farther into the dense foliage.

When the sounds of the pursuers grew louder, they both went completely still.

"Where the hell did they disappear?" one of the men said.

Sounds like three men. The one who captured me must have joined the others again.

"You beat the bushes around here. We'll keep going. Widen the search."

They're splitting up.

Maybe that's good. Maybe we can take at least one of them out.

He thought of a plan, telling Elizabeth what he had in mind.

He could feel her uncertainty but also her determination.

He took up a position behind a tree, and she moved into a patch of low bushes.

"Matt," she called out. "Matt, I'm stuck. Help me."

Two of the men were too far away to hear her. The other stopped at once, reversing direction and moving cautiously toward the spot where she was standing.

Matt tensed, waiting for the guy to get closer.

"All right," the thug called out. "I see you. Come out with your hands up."

Elizabeth moaned. "My foot's stuck."

The man took a few careful steps closer, and Matt struck, sending out a bolt that hit him squarely in the center of the chest. He went down, and they both crouched over him.

Matt removed the football helmet and inspected the

inside. There was some kind of heavy foil lining, and he laughed out loud.

"What?"

"You know some paranoid mental patients think aluminum foil will protect them from outside influences probing their brains? Apparently it works—at least when we're the ones doing the probing."

The man was stirring. When he reached up and found that his helmet was gone, he gasped.

"Who are you? Why are you after us?" Matt asked.

"Following orders."

"Who wants us? And why?"

"I'm just doing a job," he said, repeating what the other guy had said.

"And why are you wearing a helmet?"

"The boss said to."

"Why?"

He looked away. "He said you had some kind of mind control rays."

Oh, great.

Too bad we can't read minds, Elizabeth said.

Too bad he doesn't have more information. But we can't waste a lot of time on him. The others could come back. He bent to the man. *Stop looking for us. Go back to your car. Drive away.*

The man looked confused.

Go on. Get out of here, before the man and woman do something worse to you.

The man gave them a panicked look. Pushing himself up, he began running back the way he'd come as if the devil were after him.

When he was out of sight, Matt and Elizabeth moved farther into the swamp. Ahead of them, Matt saw one of the bayous that cut through the area. They could run along the edge, or they could plunge in—which might or might not be a good idea, depending on whether an alligator was waiting to scoop them up.

In the distance, he saw a pier sticking out into the brown water. A couple boats were moored there.

Elizabeth followed his thoughts, and they both ran for the dock.

Behind them they could hear running feet. When a bullet whizzed past them, Matt whirled and returned fire, making the attackers duck into the underbrush.

That gave them a little time, but he knew he and Elizabeth would be sitting ducks when they went out onto the dock.

He slowed, trying to make a decision. *I'm going first.*

That didn't work out so well last time.

What's your suggestion?

We go into the water on the other side of the dock and climb into one of the boats.

Risky. But may be our only option. You go in. I'll hold them off.

They reached the pier, and both ducked to the other side. He took up a position at the end near the shore, ready to stop the bad guys from coming closer. Elizabeth went into the water, swimming along the pier where she was sheltered from the men who were coming cautiously through the trees.

From behind the cover of the dock, Matt got off a couple shots at the pursuers, making them think twice about coming closer. But the standoff couldn't last forever. There were still two pursuers left, and Matt had only the ammunition in the one weapon.

As he kept part of his focus on the men, he also followed Elizabeth's progress. She made it to one of the crafts, a speedboat with an inboard motor.

This one?

He answered in the affirmative, wishing he knew more about boats. But they had to get out of a bad situation, and the vessel seemed to be their best alternative.

Can you get in it?

I hope so.

It had seemed like a good idea at the time, but making it from the water into the boat was easier said than done. As she tried to heave herself over the side, he waited with his breath shallow in his lungs, wishing he could swim over and boost her up. But he had to stay where he was, holding off the pursuers.

ELIZABETH STRUGGLED TO pull herself inside, but it was clear that the side of the craft was too high for her to scramble over from her position in the water. Her only alternative was to set the boat rocking from side to side. When it was almost dipping into the water, she finally flopped over the gunwale, onto the bench seats, banging her hip and shoulder as she came down.

Wet and dripping, she lay there for a few moments, struggling to pull her thoughts together.

Now what?

You have to start it.

She began searching around, looking for a key. It wasn't under the dashboard, and it wasn't in any of the compartments around the craft.

Zap it. Like I zapped the door lock in the basement of The Mansion.

This is a little different.

She made a low sound, but began studying the controls, and Matt directed her to the starter.

She focused on it, giving it a mental jolt, then another. Nothing happened, and she thought they might have to abandon the craft and go to plan B—which was swimming across the bayou and disappearing into the swamp beyond—if they could make it across without getting shot before an alligator ate them.

When she was about to give up hope of starting the boat, the engine coughed, then sprang to life.

Good work.

TO KEEP THE THUGS from rushing forward, Matt got off a couple more shots. Then the gun clicked and he knew he was out of bullets. Abandoning his position at the side of the dock, he leaped up on the boards. As soon as he made a run up the boat, the bad guys started shooting. He ducked low, and he heard a gasp behind him. In his mind's eye, he saw what was happening. Elizabeth had turned and was hurling bolts of power at the men, pushing them out of range, giving him time to untie the boat from the piling and leap inside.

Elizabeth watched him jump aboard, then turned back to the wheel. As she pulled away, the men started shooting again. He and Elizabeth bent low, making themselves as small a target as possible while the craft roared up the bayou.

Matt looked back at the two men. One of them seemed to be in charge and was giving orders to the other. He pointed toward another motorboat moored nearby, and they ran to the vessel and jumped in.

Matt was pretty sure they weren't going to make the engine turn over with their minds. But it seemed they didn't need to. When he heard the craft start, he muttered a curse. Either they knew where to find the key or they had lucked out.

He cursed again as the boat took off after them, and it became clear very quickly that the other craft was more powerful.

"They're gaining on us. What are we going to do?" she shouted. "Can we goose up the engine?"

"I don't know."

He focused on the motor, trying to force it to put out more speed, but the maneuver didn't seem to be working, and all they could do was keep going.

The men in the boat behind them kept firing their guns, the shots becoming more accurate the closer they got. Bullets whizzed past, and some struck the hull. Matt looked down, seeing water rising in the bottom of the boat. They were sinking.

Chapter Twenty-One

"We have to bail out," he said. "Then dive below the surface and swim toward shore."

"No, wait." Elizabeth pointed toward a blue van that had turned onto the road beside the bayou and was racing along, keeping pace with the two boats.

He gave her a questioning look.

"It's them."

"Who?"

"The woman I told you about. The one who was prob-ing my mind."

"Is that good or bad?"

"I don't know."

From the van, a voice zinged toward them. *We're here to help. We're going to blow up the other boat. Add your energy to ours.*

Matt still couldn't be sure that the people in the van were on their side, but he knew for sure that the men in the other boat were closing in for the kill.

He looked toward the van, trying to see who was inside. Someone slid a window open, and he saw several people.

With a little prayer that he was making the right move, he fed power to the woman in the van.

He felt her building energy, and then a beam of tremen-dous force shot from the van to the pursuing boat.

For a moment it seemed to hover in the water. Then the gas tank exploded with an enormous boom. The boat disintegrated, sending a shock wave across the water, and swamping Matt and Elizabeth's craft. They went into the water, both of them gasping for air as waves from the shattered craft pounded them.

Elizabeth, Matt cried out in his mind. When she didn't answer, everything inside him went cold.

Still shell-shocked from the explosion, he tried to focus, tried to figure out where she was. At first he heard nothing. Then he picked up dim echoes from her mind. She was underwater, unconscious and sinking.

He dragged in a breath and held it, diving below the surface, swimming toward where he thought she was.

He could see nothing in the murky water, but he kept going, guided by his connection to her. His own lungs felt like they would burst, but he stayed under, because if Elizabeth died, he might as well die with her.

But finally, finally, his searching hand hit against her shoulder. He grabbed her shirt, trying to summon the strength to pull them both up. Then he realized that another man was beside him, grasping Elizabeth's other side and helping pull her upward.

They broke the surface, and Matt gasped for breath.

They pulled Elizabeth to shore and laid her on the bank. She was pale and lifeless, and Matt checked her airways before turning her over and starting to press the water from her lungs.

Water gushed from her mouth, and he screamed in his mind as he worked, *Elizabeth. For God's sake, Elizabeth.*

For horrible moments, she failed to respond. And then he caught a glimmer of consciousness.

He kept calling to her, saying her name, telling her how much he loved her.

Matt?

Right here.

What happened?

They blew up the other boat, and you went down.

He turned her over, clasping her to him, ignoring the crowd that had gathered around them. But finally their voices penetrated his own consciousness.

"Thank God."

"I'm so sorry. I didn't know that would happen." That was the woman who had directed the energy beam at the other boat.

"It's all right. You kept them from shooting us." That last comment came from Elizabeth, who was taking in the men and women around them.

You're like us, she marveled.

Yes. And we have to get out of here before someone comes to investigate the explosion.

Was it safe to go with them? Matt wondered.

Yes, Elizabeth answered, and he let her faith guide him.

The men and women helped them to the van. Like the night at The Mansion. Cold and wet in a van.

Matt pulled Elizabeth closer and tried to pay attention to where they were going, but it was still hard to focus. He knew that they stopped at a shopping center. Some of the newcomers stayed in the van. Others went in and bought dry clothing. First the men cleared out and Elizabeth changed in the van. Then it was Matt's turn.

The dry clothing did wonders for him, and he looked around at the people who had rescued them.

"How did you find us?" he asked.

"Rachel found you," one of the men answered. "We're all children who were born as a result of Douglas Solomon's experiments—using fertilized human eggs he acquired from his fertility clinic."

"We found out from Maven Bolton that he was trying to make superintelligent children," Matt said. "And, instead, he got us."

There were murmurs of agreement.

"And we are…what, exactly?" Matt asked.

"You probably figured that out, too. Telepaths who couldn't connect with anyone on a deep level until we met someone else from the clinic," one of the women said. "I'm Rachel Harper."

In turn, they all gave their names.

Jake Harper, Stephanie Branson, Craig Branson, Gabriella Boudreaux, Luke Buckley.

"You were probing my mind," Elizabeth said to Rachel. "When we were driving down here."

"I'm sorry if I alarmed you."

"Why did you do it?"

"Because we had to be sure you weren't enemies. The first time we met other people who had been altered by the clinic, they tried to kill us."

"Why?" Elizabeth gasped.

"They were selfish. They wanted to be the only ones with special powers."

"Nice," Matt murmured.

They turned onto an access road, then drew up in front of what looked like a large plantation house. "This is where I grew up," the woman named Gabriella said. "I've opened a restaurant here, but it's closed today. We can all go inside and relax."

Matt was still overwhelmed to meet this group of people.

We're on your side, Rachel Harper said.

Matt swung toward her. *Got to watch what I think.*

We all do. That's one of the little inconvenient things about us. But I know you've been practicing blocking your thoughts. You'll get better at it.

Inside Gabriella led the way upstairs to a sitting room on the second floor.

Matt and Elizabeth sat together, still coming to terms with their narrow escape.

"Who was after us?" he asked.

"We can't be sure who he was. Dr. Solomon is dead. And so is a man named Bill Wellington, who funded the project through a Washington think tank called the Howell Institute. That should have laid the past to rest. But it appears that someone else knew about children from the clinic. Either they knew what was going on back then—or perhaps they discovered it."

"Why were they chasing us? What do they want?" Elizabeth asked.

"They're after us because of what we are," Jake answered. "We've got powers they don't understand. Which makes us a threat, or maybe an asset that someone can exploit. Like a secret weapon."

Elizabeth shuddered.

"You have to admit that being able to send mental bolts of power at your enemies is a skill to covet."

Matt nodded.

"It's a lot to deal with," Rachel said. "And I'm sure the two of you want some time alone to think about what you're going to do."

"What are our choices?" Matt asked.

"You can stay here with us. Or you can go off on your own. It's up to you."

Elizabeth looked at Rachel. "You have a shop in the French Quarter. Where you do tarot-card readings."

"Yes."

"I went there. I mean, I was drawn there by..." She lifted a shoulder. "I don't know. I guess there was some kind of connection between us."

"I'm sorry I wasn't in town. It would have avoided that boat chase."

"Yeah, but the guys in the other boat would still be alive," Jake said in a hard voice. "It worked out."

Matt looked at him and knew that it was a lot better to be friends with Jake Harper than his enemy.

Jake answered with a small nod.

They talked for a while longer, each couple telling how they'd met and what had happened to them as a result.

Finally Gabriella said, "You must be worn out. There's an empty cottage on the property. Why don't the two of you go over there and relax? And we can all meet back here for dinner." She looked at her watch. "At six-thirty."

"Yes. Thanks," Elizabeth said.

Gabriella showed them to the vacant cottage.

Elizabeth looked around admiringly at the antique pieces and classic fabrics. "It's charming."

"Stephanie's the one with the visual smarts," Gabriella said. "She did the decorating, but we've all been going to country auctions and estate sales—picking up furniture for here and the main house."

Elizabeth nodded.

"I'll leave you alone."

When Gabriella had walked out of the cottage and closed the door behind her, Matt turned to Elizabeth.

"In my wildest dreams, I didn't imagine anything like this," she whispered. "People like us. Friends."

"Yeah. And the two of us—safe at last."

He reached for her, and they embraced. He wanted to take her straight to the bedroom, but they were still covered with dried bayou water.

She grinned at him, and he knew what she had in mind. They both headed for the shower, discarding their clothing as they reached the bathroom.

Matt turned on the water, adjusted the temperature and stepped under the spray. Elizabeth followed, and he reached for the soap, slicking his hands and running them over her bottom, her hips and up to her breasts.

She made an appreciative sound, leaning in to him as she soaped her own hands and caressed his back and butt, then clasped his erection, stroking up and down, making him gasp.

"Not like this," he muttered.

"You don't like it?"

"You know I do."

She turned him loose, and they kissed as they washed off the soap.

When she reached for the shampoo and began to lather his hair, he groaned at the delay. But he saw the smile in her mind.

Foreplay.

Are you trying to drive me crazy?

I'm enjoying the freedom I never thought we'd have.

Oh, yeah.

He returned the favor, washing her hair. They'd barely rinsed off when he scooped her up in his arms, cradling her against him as he fitted her body to his. Leaning back against the wall, he let her do most of the work, and they climaxed together in a burst of sensations. As he eased her down, she melted against him, and they stood under the rushing water, spent but happy.

When the shower began to cool, he turned off the taps. Both of them were almost too limp to move, but they managed to dry off and hold each other up as they staggered to the bedroom.

Under the covers, they cleaved together. Two people who had always been alone. But no longer.

The events of the day had taken their toll, and they were both quickly asleep.

SOME TIME LATER, Elizabeth woke and marveled at the way she felt. Safe and relaxed and free.

For the first time since she'd crashed into that light pole, no one was trying to kill her. *I'm still overwhelmed that we found each other.*

Yes. And it's not just the two of us. There are people who understand us.

She nodded against Matt's shoulder, taking in his thoughts, catching the edge of his sudden tension. Even though she knew what he was thinking, she also knew he was going to say it aloud.

He pushed himself up in the bed, and she did the same, pulling the covers up with her.

He cleared his throat and looked at her. "I'm finally free to ask. Will you marry me?"

"You know I will."

Reaching for her, he folded her into his arms, and they clung together.

"Being with you is a dream come true," she murmured.

"But it's real. And it's the beginning of our lives together."

She sensed another thought in his mind. "Getting married is a good idea before we have kids."

"You want them?" he asked.

"Yes, even though it makes me a little nervous. What powers will they have?"

"I guess we'll find out," he said.

"They won't be alone the way we were. They'll have us."

"Yes. And we have to make sure they have a safe place to grow up."

"Like here," she breathed.

"You want to stay here?"

"I think so. I feel so blessed that Rachel and the others found us." She squeezed his hand. "We should get dressed and go over to dinner—before they wonder where we are."

"They know," he answered. "But they're giving us privacy. They know how much we love each other. And they know we're going to want a lot of time alone."

He grinned at her, and she followed his thoughts.

"Not just for sex." She said it aloud.

"Of course not."

They climbed out of bed and began to dress, both of them loving the freedom to joke around and the freedom to plan the rest of their lives together.

* * * * *

REQUEST YOUR FREE BOOKS!
2 FREE NOVELS PLUS 2 FREE GIFTS!

HARLEQUIN

INTRIGUE

BREATHTAKING ROMANTIC SUSPENSE

YES! Please send me 2 FREE Harlequin Intrigue® novels and my 2 FREE gifts (gifts are worth about $10). After receiving them, if I don't wish to receive any more books, I can return the shipping statement marked "cancel." If I don't cancel, I will receive 6 brand-new novels every month and be billed just $4.74 per book in the U.S. or $5.24 per book in Canada. That's a savings of at least 14% off the cover price! It's quite a bargain! Shipping and handling is just 50¢ per book in the U.S. and 75¢ per book in Canada.* I understand that accepting the 2 free books and gifts places me under no obligation to buy anything. I can always return a shipment and cancel at any time. Even if I never buy another book, the two free books and gifts are mine to keep forever.

182/382 HDN F42N

Name _____ (PLEASE PRINT)

Address _____ Apt. #

City _____ State/Prov. _____ Zip/Postal Code

Signature (if under 18, a parent or guardian must sign)

Mail to the Harlequin® Reader Service:
IN U.S.A.: P.O. Box 1867, Buffalo, NY 14240-1867
IN CANADA: P.O. Box 609, Fort Erie, Ontario L2A 5X3
Are you a subscriber to Harlequin Intrigue books
and want to receive the larger-print edition?
Call 1-800-873-8635 or visit www.ReaderService.com.

* Terms and prices subject to change without notice. Prices do not include applicable taxes. Sales tax applicable in N.Y. Canadian residents will be charged applicable taxes. Offer not valid in Quebec. This offer is limited to one order per household. Not valid for current subscribers to Harlequin Intrigue books. All orders subject to credit approval. Credit or debit balances in a customer's account(s) may be offset by any other outstanding balance owed by or to the customer. Please allow 4 to 6 weeks for delivery. Offer available while quantities last.

Your Privacy—The Harlequin® Reader Service is committed to protecting your privacy. Our Privacy Policy is available online at www.ReaderService.com or upon request from the Harlequin Reader Service.

We make a portion of our mailing list available to reputable third parties that offer products we believe may interest you. If you prefer that we not exchange your name with third parties, or if you wish to clarify or modify your communication preferences, please visit us at www.ReaderService.com/consumerchoice or write to us at Harlequin Reader Service Preference Service, P.O. Box 9062, Buffalo, NY 14269. Include your complete name and address.

HI13R

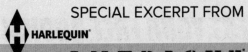
SAWYER
by USA TODAY *bestselling author*
Delores Fossen

A woman he'd spent one incredible night with and the baby who could be his will have Agent Sawyer Ryland fighting for a future he never imagined…

Agent Sawyer Ryland caught the movement from the corner of his eye, turned and saw the blonde pushing her way through the other guests who'd gathered for the wedding reception.

She wasn't hard to spot.

She was practically running, and she had a bundle of something gripped in front of her like a shield.

Sawyer's pulse kicked up a notch, and he automatically slid his hand inside his jacket and over his Glock. It was sad that his first response was to pull his firearm even at his own brother's wedding reception. Still, he'd been an FBI agent long enough—and had been shot too many times—that he lived by the code of better safe than sorry.

Or better safe than dead.

She stopped in the center of the barn that'd been decorated with hundreds of clear twinkling lights and flowers, and even though she was wearing dark sunglasses, Sawyer was pretty sure that her gaze rifled around. Obviously looking for someone. However, the looking around skidded to a halt when her attention landed on him.

"Sawyer," she said.

HIEXP69758

Because of the chattering guests and the fiddler sawing out some bluegrass, Sawyer didn't actually hear her speak his name. Instead, he saw it shape her trembling mouth. She yanked off the sunglasses, her gaze colliding with his.

"Cassidy O'Neal," he mumbled.

Yeah, it was her all right. Except she didn't much look like a pampered princess doll today in her jeans and body-swallowing gray T-shirt.

Despite the fact that he wasn't giving off any welcoming vibes whatsoever, Cassidy hurried to him. Her mouth was still trembling. Her dark green eyes rapidly blinking. There were beads of sweat on her forehead and upper lip despite the half dozen or so massive fans circulating air into the barn.

"I'm sorry," she said, and she thrust whatever she was carrying at him.

Sawyer didn't take it and backed up, but not before he caught a glimpse of the tiny hand gripping the white blanket.

A baby.

That put his heart right in his suddenly dry throat.

*To find out what happens,
don't miss* USA TODAY *bestselling author
Delores Fossen's SAWYER, on sale in May 2014,
wherever Harlequin® Intrigue® books are sold!*

HIEXP69758

INTRIGUE

**IN THE CITY BY THE BAY,
THE TRUTH WILL COME OUT...**

A body left in the woods, marked by a killer...
and it wasn't the first. The quicker Special Agent
Christina Sandoval brought this serial killer to justice, the
sooner she'd get back to her daughter. Reason enough
for the FBI to have sent her partner...who was also her
ex-fiancé, Eric Brody. While Brody's sense of justice never
failed, his relationship with Sandoval had. The deeper
they dug into the case, the more personal it got. With an
elusive killer that seemed to know more about Christina
than Brody ever did, they'd both need to stop holding
back, or be the next to fall victim to this private war.

THE DISTRICT

BY CAROL ERICSON

*Only from Harlequin® Intrigue®.
Available May 2014 wherever books are sold.*

HI69759